DON'T TOUCH ME

A jewel heist goes wrong when the escaping robbers abduct Gloria Vane, the beautiful film actress. Then as gang leader Ace Monohan falls for Gloria, it leads to dissension amongst his men, and the destruction and abandonment of his hideout. Ace, forced to go on the run, takes the stolen jewels with him. Now Gloria finds herself at the mercy of rival gangster 'Fingers' Baxter, who plans to use her to lure Ace out of hiding . . .

JOHN RUSSELL FEARN

DON'T TOUCH ME

Complete and Unabridged

LINFORD
Leicester

First published in Great Britain

First Linford Edition
published 2009

British Library CIP Data

Fearn, John Russell, *1908 – 1960*
    Don't touch me.—Large print ed.—
Linford mystery library
    1. Gangsters—Fiction
    2. Detective and mystery stories
    3. Large type books
    I. Title
    823.9'12 [F]

ISBN 978–1–84782–524–7

Published by
F. A. Thorpe (Publishing)
Anstey, Leicestershire

Set by Words & Graphics Ltd.
Anstey, Leicestershire
Printed and bound in Great Britain by
T. J. International Ltd., Padstow, Cornwall

This book is printed on acid-free paper

1

'Filanti's Saloon,' Al Dyson said. He peered out of the rear window of the black Chevrolet as it came to a halt. 'They sure give these joints some monickers. Why don't they call it a rock pile an' ha' done with it?'

'It's 'salon' — mug!'

Ace Monohan sat motionless after he'd spoken. The big jewelry store matched up with the movie and still photographs he'd had taken of it. He knew as much about the building as the architects. He had to.

Besides Ace himself — short, powerfully-built, swarthily dark, flashily-dressed — there were five other men in the car, including bonehead Al Dyson. Each one of them waited, tight-lipped, ready for action.

'You mugs all set?' Ace asked abruptly. 'None of you feel like takin' a powder?'

'Guess not, boss.'

The driver said: 'I got everything doped out, Ace.'

'Okay — now a quick run-through before we get movin'. You keep your engine runnin', Jimmy — an' monkey around with the dash, as though you're tryin' to find something wrong. That'll make things look good if the cops come nosin' around — though from my schedule, it ain't likely any of 'em will. Right so far?'

Jimmy made an 'O' of his finger and thumb.

Ace finished: 'The rest of you come with me. Once we got what we want, we get outa town quick — over George Washington Bridge to New Jersey. After that, we hit the State road for Penn., and that should put us in the clear. Okay for gas, Jimmy?'

'Sure thing.'

Ace thought of something. His dark eyes pinned his followers.

'Get this straight — no shootin'! Use your hardware to hold up the joint, sure — but don't plug anybody. That kind of rap's too tough to break. Don't crash in like you're goin' to a fancy hop — just take it calm, and leave me to do the talkin'.'

He climbed out of the car on to the sidewalk and surveyed. He lit a cigarette, so it gave him time to check up. Nobody was around who mattered — just one or two men and women, mugs who worked for a living. Nobody else. Ace set his black homburg at a sharper angle and pushed open the store's gleaming glass and chromium doors.

About six people were inside, making no noise on inch-thick pile carpet. Showcases with hard glass tops were standing around, like so many coffins. Al Dyson swallowed hard behind his butterfly bow. The place was ripe for plucking.

Ace moved. A girl moved at the same time from a little way off. She was twentyish, with snug hips and full breasts. Her dress looked like it was glued on Black, sure — but that didn't stop it showing what kind of shape she was in. She had yellow hair, baby blue eyes, and smelled elegant.

'Anything I can do for you, gentlemen?'

she asked, with the sort of smile that goes with a tooth-ad.

'You kiddin'?' Ace asked dryly, as his eyes darted beyond her to the two other women and one man assistant, all of them dealing with customers.

'If you would like — '

'I'd like you to keep your trap shut, sister.' Ace said, his voice low.

The girl blinked. Ace grinned at her and showed strong white teeth round his smoldering cigarette. For a moment, she figured he was joking, until she glanced down at something hard jabbed just under her left breast.

'Keep your arms down.' Ace murmured. 'Show any sign that this is a stick-up, kid, and there'll be a lily in your hand. Just act normal. Nobody can see this rod 'cept you an' me. Just talk to me nicely, see?'

'I — er — ' The girl stared fixedly, baffled. Ace grinned and looked her up and down.

'Pity I'm busy,' he said. 'You've got lines I could go nuts about — ' He jerked his head to his colleagues and they began moving. Ace remained where he was. He shifted his gun from the salesgirl so that it covered the others in the salon.

'Take it easy, folks!' he snapped out. 'This is the real thing. Don't try anythin', and nobody'll get hurt.'

Everybody remained motionless, like they were frozen — then, after a second or two, the left foot of the manager began to stray to a floor alarm push under the carpet.

Ace asked coldly. 'You lookin' to be a cripple, fella? Move that foot any further, an' I'll blast it from under you.'

The manager froze again. Ace drew at his cigarette, dividing his attention between the activity of his boys and the full lines of the girl beside him.

'Know me, sweetheart?' he asked her, and he didn't look at her. His eyes were shuttling back and forth from the calm sidewalk to his boys.

'You're Monohan,' she answered. 'A no-account gangster, who has been on the run for about eighteen months. I've seen your picture in the papers.'

'It wasn't a good one,' Ace told her. 'I

ain't that bad-lookin'. But this is just to warn you, kid. Describe me to anybody when this is over — or talk about my boys, either — and I guess you'll be givin' a mortician a job. Just keep quiet.'

The salesgirl didn't say anything, but her eyes strayed from Ace's square, bulldog face to his right hand. The first finger on it was queer — flattened, as though somebody had stepped on it when it was made.

'Okay, boss,' Al said abruptly, as he and the men finished frisking the joint. 'Guess we got all we need.'

Ace gave a look around and nodded. He started to talk again.

'There's something you folks had better get straight right now. You know what all of us look like. That's 'cos we couldn't mask ourselves when we had to cross the sidewalk to get in here. It'd have been a natural tip-off, see? Sooner take the risk of you folk talking — ' Ace studied each one intently in turn. 'But if you do talk, it'll be just too bad,' he finished. 'I can aim straight — an' fast. So can my boys. Better remember that, huh?'

Nobody said anything. Ace grinned and brought his hand down on the salesgirl's buttocks.

'Remind me to look you up some time,' he said: then he wheeled and dived for the door with his boys behind him.

All of them were across the sidewalk and in the sedan in three seconds flat. The doors shammed as the car swept away from the kerb, shaving the head-lamps of a car coming in the opposite direction.

'Get everythin'?' Ace demanded, and his dark eyes glanced sharply through the window.

'Sure did,' Al told him. 'Not far from two hundred grand. We just shoveled in trays of the stuff like you told us — ' and he patted the two hide suitcases on the floor at his feet.

'Nice goin.' Ace leaned forward and spoke to the driver: 'Say, Jimmy, keep on goin' on the route we mapped out — an' don't try jumpin' the lights. Make for George Washington Bridge as fast as you can. What about the number plates?'

'Switched,' Jimmy said, twisting the big

car in and out of the swirling traffic. 'Just like you said — ' And he nodded to a caliper-like lever on the steering column with which the turning of the front and rear plates had been accomplished.

'I feel better,' Ace decided, and sat back to light another cigarette. 'Everythin' goin' like we planned it. Those mugs back at the store'll raise the alarm, sure — but we'll be in the clear by then. If we're stopped we're on a fishin' trip, see? We'll ditch the cases in the floor trapdoor here. They'll be safe on the axle shaft. I had Baldy fix a nice little wooden nest for 'em to drop in. Everythin' taken care of — 'cept one thing.'

The men around him looked startled. He grinned at them.

'Nothin' serious. I'd just have liked the time to see more of that dame with the yellow hair. Be a swell number in a tumble, I guess. She smelled kinda cute, too.'

Al gave a sour look. 'Listen, Ace, if any cops stop us, they'll know who we are. Our pusses are well known everywhere. They won't swallow that fishin' trip routine — an' you know it.'

'Mebbe not, but even a cop can't do anything without proof, an' that can only come from identification. None of those lily-whites back at the salon will take that chance. I'm gambling on it.'

'Mind you ain't in the red,' Al growled, and sat back again.

Ace looked dangerous for a moment, then he relaxed and went on smoking placidly. His nerves were edgy, though. He'd never pulled a robbery so barefaced as this one — but he hadn't planned the getaway so thoroughly before, either. Chances were even on getting clear. Jimmy was probably the coolest; as driver, he had to be. He didn't jump the signals; he kept within speed limits — but, where he could manage it, he opened out and skimmed along dizzily, slicing corners and hugging short routes.

From Fifth Avenue, he took the car round the north end of Central Park and then ducked down the side alleys until he came to the welcome sight of the George Washington Bridge. He drove over it and into New Jersey.

Once he was away from the more crowded regions, Jimmy began to give the speedometer some exercise.

'Begins to look like we made it,' Ace commented. 'I reckon there isn't anythin' to stop us goin' all out to Scranton. We can ditch the car there an' change to a blue convertible. I've gotten it all fixed. After that it's straight ahead for Loyalsock. We can lie there until the heat's off, then I'll contact that fence in Harrisburg to come over an' talk business.'

None of them spoke. Most of them weren't listening to Ace, anyway; they had their ears cocked for the sound of police sirens — but none came.

The speedometer crept up. sixty — sixty-five — seventy. Jimmy gave the big car its head and, with the soft whine of tires on macadam, the sedan hurtled over the miles. The sprawling outskirts of the city faded to the rear. There was open country ahead, sunny in the June morning. Emptiness — Scranton — and safety.

Then, suddenly, the distant wailing of a police car siren. Ace twirled and stared through the rear window. Remotely, but growing bigger with the seconds there was the vision of a speed cop. Jimmy looked into the rear mirror.

'Stop, boss — or ditch him?' he asked briefly.

'Neither,' Ace snapped. 'He's not tailin' us for that hold-up: It's our speed that's gettin' in his hair. No police cars are followin', so we don't need to stay an' be pleasant. Lose him, Jimmy — an' fast.'

'Oke.'

Though the car was already going hell-for-leather; it put on a spurt. There was nothing to stop it. Straight road, no corners — yet. Seventy-five — seventy-eight — eighty-five. The wind roared against the car, the treads of the tires made a high-pitched whistle. The pursuing speed-cop became smaller and his siren less audible.

'That lane ahead,' Ace said abruptly. 'There — turning left. Get in it, quick. We can duck him that way — '

The steering wheel flew round. Going at the speed he was, Jimmy did not dare brake sharply. He slackened for a fraction of a second, plunging the nose of the car round. Hedges danced crazily across the sky as the lane swung like a zig-zag white line in front. It was shrouded in dust. Something was coming out of it. Red, fairly big —

It slammed straight into the sedan with an impact that slewed it sideways, over and over, and then down the embankment skirting the lane.

Ace realized that he was turning somersaults, hitting the sides and floor. He landed with the crushing weight of two men on top of him. He wasn't dead, but he was mightily bruised. Groaning and swearing, he dragged himself from the tangled-up mess of men and cushions. The car hadn't caught fire, even though it lay on one side.

It was smashed to hell. Ace could see that as he looked at the ruin around him. Jimmy was dead, impaled by the broken crosspiece of the steering wheel. He sat at a ridiculous horizontal angle, grinning like a damned fool, with blood trickling from the corners of his mouth.

'Hell,' Ace whispered, wincing as he

moved his battered legs. 'Sufferin' hell.'

He pulled himself to the door. It was half open, sprung by the impact. He reached the grass. Al, and then one more of his boys, followed him. They lay gasping, streaked with blood, yet alive. They began to look around them.

'I guess — Jimmy overdid it,' Al panted, pulling the back of his hand over his mouth. 'He cornered too quickly — looks like he got the works, too, same as Slats an' Baldy — ' and he nodded to the smashed bodies of the two other men who had been with Jimmy in the front seat.

'Yeah — ' Ace got up unsteadily, his clothes in rags. 'But it wasn't just cornerin' that did this. We hit sump'n. I saw it coming — '

He looked about him in the dispersing dust. Everything seemed unnaturally quiet. Even the police-cop had vanished. Probably he had never thought anybody could corner into the side road at that speed. In any case, the sedan was deep down the embankment, and hidden from the top by bushes and long grass. In the distance, the main road traffic followed its undisturbed way.

'Take a look,' Al gasped abruptly, and the grip he gave Ace's arm made him turn from surveying the distant main road to look at a red coupé standing on its roof a dozen yards away. One of its front wheels was still revolving slowly in the misty dust.

'That was it,' Ace snapped. 'The blasted thing I saw coming. Some fool driver on the wrong side.'

He forgot to add Jimmy had been way over on the wrong side, too, and stumbled forward. Lying flat, he peered inside the coupé and then gave a start. He saw a girl's leg shapely enough, with a laddered nylon encasing it.

'A dame.' Al exclaimed, looking intently. 'And knocked out cold from the looks of her.'

She was. Ace wriggled his way into the narrow cavity where she lay. She was not pinned down by any part of the car, but a monstrous bruise across her white forehead showed where she'd taken it.

'Swell looker,' said Steve Moran,

coming up behind Al to survey the proceedings. He was big, ugly, but reliable. Only fate could explain why he'd been allowed to survive with his two equally unworthy companions.

'Never mind how she looks,' Ace snapped, from inside the car. 'Help me get her out.'

'What for?' Al demanded. 'We ain't got time to be messin' about with this dame. Leave her be. She'll come round.'

'Shut up! For one thing, I like the looks of her, and for another, she'll talk a lot when she does come round, and that'll only make things more difficult for us. Don't forget our sedan's back there with the trick number plates on it, and there ain't nothin' we can do to alter 'em. I want to be sure of this baby, whoever she is. Grab her feet, Al, an' pull.'

Al grabbed and pulled — and didn't look happy about it. Not that he objected to holding the unknown girl's ankles, but because he knew dames and robberies never mixed. No use telling that to Ace, though. He'd always been a sucker for a pretty face.

And the girl was pretty — no doubt about it. Bit pale now; the make-up smudged. Ace kneeled and looked at her as, his hands rubbing her wrists, she presently stirred and opened very wide, smoke-gray eyes. She had long, curling lashes that were natural.

'Okay, kid, take it easy,' Ace said briefly. 'You're safe enough. I reckon we — '

'You — you drove right into me!' she exclaimed, rising up; then she swayed a little and fingered the bruise on her forehead. 'I wasn't doing more than fifteen — '

She stopped, and Ace wondered why. Then he knew, and gave a start. Al and Steve Moran knew the reason also, at the same moment. The girl was looking fixedly at the two suitcases nearby. The lids had sprung open, so the insides of the cases were visible. One was half empty; the other glittered in the sunlight like something out of Monte Christo's haul.

'That's a lot of jewelry,' the girl said, and her smoke-gray eyes moved to Ace.

'Yeah — I'm a traveler.' He grinned through his cut lips and then stood up, aiming a look at Al and Steve. They turned to the cases and began searching around for whatever had fallen out of them.

'Sure you're not a thief — all of you?' The girl had a very direct but pleasing voice, and she spoke as if she earned a living out of it.

'I said I was a traveler.' Ace gave her a grim look

'Travelers don't go about with stuff as good as that.'

Al closed up the two cases. He was not sure whether everything had been retrieved. Probably not. Have to be content. He looked at the girl grimly, then back to Ace.

'All right — all right — I know what you're thinking,' Ace told him. 'You ain't got no need to worry. The girl's coming along with us. Now mebbe you're glad we dug her out?'

'I am not!' Al snapped. 'Knocked out as she was, we could have gotten away with it.'

Ace said nothing. He watched as the girl got to her feet. She smoothed her dusty rumpled two-piece slowly and stood looking at the shattered sedan. She went over to it, stared in horror for a moment at the dead men in the front, then looked at the registration plates. She wheeled round, her eyes bright.

'I was right. You are crooks! These are false number plates, with a gadget to work 'em. I've seen such things in the movies.'

'See what I mean?' Ace asked, looking at Al. 'Picks things up nice an' natural, don't she?' He went over to her and seized her arm. 'All right, sister, so we made a snatch — an' we did take some rocks. But I don't aim to let you talk about it. It wouldn't be nice.'

'You can't hold me!' she flared at him. 'Who do you think you are? You wouldn't dare. I — I amount to something. People will be looking for me.'

'Yeah? How much do you amount to? I'll tell you what I think of the price.'

'I'm Gloria Vane. I'm a movie actress. I was on my way to see my New York agent when you collided with me.'

Ace looked at her. Now her color was

coming back she was even more good-looking than he'd figured. From the look of things, her hair wasn't peroxided, either. Nature had been generous in feature and figure.

'Never heard of Gloria Vane.' Al said bluntly. 'An' it ain't 'cos I don't go to the movies. I'm there in my off time.'

'I'm not a big-time actress.' Gloria Vane said. 'I wish I were — just small parts. But I'm pretty good, and I — '

'I don't want your life history, sister,' Ace interrupted her. 'All I'm interested in right now is that you know more than's good for you. That being so, you need an escort — an' you're gettin' it. I'm going to look after you for a while, see? Just till you're rested up.'

'You try it!' she blazed. 'What right have you to — '

'Every right, when you're a danger.' Ace tugged out his Luger from his torn jacket. 'I'm taking no chances. You can't argue with this hardware, kid, so don't start trying.'

Gloria breathed hard. Ace stood looking at her, admiring her beauty.

'You can't get ten yards trying to abduct me,' she said at length. 'And you know what the penalty is for kidnapping.'

'This ain't kidnapping,' Ace told her. 'You're coming of your own free will, 'cos if you don't, you'll get a slug between them pretty shoulder blades of yours, but quick.'

With an effort, Gloria got control of herself. She looked about her.

'Just what are you planning to do?'

'Get to Scranton.'

'How? Questions will be asked. We're none of us exactly dressed for a ball, are we?'

'Supposing you let me worry about that? I got contacts, you know.'

'What the dame says makes sense to me, boss,' Steve put in. 'With the car gone, and us like this, how do we keep moving?'

'I got everything figgered out,' Ace said. 'I was prepared for everything when I took on this job. I told you we were going to change to a blue convertible at Scranton, didn't I? Well, we still are. Only difference is, it'll come here an pick us up. Let me once get to a phone, an' Munro will see us in the clear in no time. That's what he's paid for.'

'And then what?' Gloria asked bitterly.

'You'll see, kid. Just keep your pretty mouth buttoned up, and you won't come to no harm. One peep outa you though and — '

Ace left the sentence unfinished. He looked at the wrecked sedan, and then the red coupé. Finally, he appeared to make up his mind about them.

'Leave 'em,' he said. 'No use settin' fire to 'em, that would only bring the cops here. Mebbe a long time before they find anything — and when they do, it won't matter. Two empty cars and three dead bodies.'

'They'll know we've gotten away,' Al pointed out. 'That'll keep the heat on. They're bound to know that there were five of us in that joint when we stuck it up.'

'I don't care what they know,' Ace retorted. 'They got to find us before they can do anything — an' they never will. An' shut up!' he finished venomously, as he saw the girl listening intently.

'You won't find it easy to swing on to me,' she said. 'As I told you, I'm liable to be looked for.'

'You're a good risk, kid. Since you're not big-time, there won't be much trouble if you're missed. You're goin' to be useful to me, 'cos you're goin' to telephone to Scranton for the car to fetch us. Won't matter if you do it; it would for Steve, or Al, or me.'

'Do you think I'd be fool enough to sign away my freedom like that?'

'Yeah — because I'll have this rod of mine trained right on you while you do it, see? I guess you're not tired of life just yet.'

The girl made no reply. Ace jerked his head.

'Get movin',' he said 'We stick on this level until we see signs of a stores. Should be one two miles off — an', while you're phonin', kid, grab off some ointment and bandages. We sure need 'em. An' Al — swing on to them cases.'

2

An hour later, the bedraggled, dusty quartet reached the outskirts of a suburban town. It was small, mostly wooden, with a gas station and a few houses thrown together. It looked as though it held the kind of people who wouldn't be curious.

Ace surveyed, and then said: 'Never mind lookin' for a drug-store. There's a garage over there — ' He nodded to the gas station near a group of sycamores at the far end of the high street. 'They'll have a phone. Get Scranton eight-two-nine-double six, an' tell Seth Munro that you're speakin' for Ace. Got that?'

Gloria sniffed. 'So that's who you are. Ace Monohan. I've read in the papers the kind of all-time heel you are.'

'Yeah? Forget it, an' tell Munro to get the blue convertible to this dump as fast as he can. Get the name of this dump, an give it to him.'

'You're plain crazy, boss,' Steve said flatly.

Ace swung on him. 'Talkin' to me, fella? Another crack like that, an' I'll pin your ears back.'

Steve said: 'Okay — if you want it that way; but I reckon we're in this as much as you. You can't trust a dame to do all that. She'll ditch us, Ace. She can call the cops.'

'Yeah — ' Ace tightened his lips. 'Yeah, could be. Guess I don't think of them things when a dame's about — like this one. Okay, I'll do the job myself and it looks like I shan't be able to get much further without risking a murder rap, amongst other things. This dame has blown my plans higher than a kite.'

He put his hand in the pocket that contained his Luger and strode across the road. To his satisfaction there was only one mechanic on duty. He came out of his glass office as he saw Ace.

'Use your phone?' Ace asked briefly.

'Yeah, sure — I guess you can.' The mechanic was looking at Ace intently.

'Somethin' wrong with me?' Ace asked sourly

'I figured you look plenty torn up, mister. What happened to you?'

'Accident. That's why I want to phone. Where is it?'

'Back there, in the office.'

Ace went through the open doorway. Then he half turned as he heard the mechanic's feet running. The guy was speeding for the big open doorways as fast as he could travel. Something had struck him, and he meant getting action. Ace hurtled after him and grabbed him before he could quite make the runway outside the garage.

'What gives?' Ace demanded, whirling the man around.

'You're Ace Monohan,' the mechanic panted. 'I've seen your face in the papers. You're a wanted man. I — '

Ace slammed out his right fist. But the mechanic was no mug. He jerked his head sideways and whipped up an uppercut which sent Ace flying back on his heels. He slipped in a pool of oil and landed with a smack that knocked the guts out of him. Then the mechanic was on top of him, pounding and slamming with his big fists.

Ace bent up his knee. It hit the mechanic in the stomach. He doubled up. Ace had no time to argue. A customer might come any minute. This lunkhead would open his trap, and then — Ace whipped out his Luger and fired. The explosion, coming from a garage, wouldn't rate anything. Probably a backfire. The mechanic put both his hands to his chest and crumpled, dropping face down on the concrete.

Ace looked about him quickly. In the garage there were half a dozen cars, including a big Buick. He raced towards it, wrenched the door open, then flung himself in the driving seat. The gas gauge said three-quarters full; the ignition key was in the lock. Ace turned it, jammed the starter, revved like hell, then whirled the big car out into the street, narrowly missing one of the pumps as he did so.

Tight-lipped, he swerved the Buick across the road in a wide circle, reached over one-handedly and snapped open the back door. Steve flung the protesting Gloria into the cushions and then fell in after her. Al came behind him and slammed the door simultaneously.

In split seconds, Ace was on his way down the high street. His driving was erratic at first, until he got the feel of the big car; then, with it under control, he gave it hell out of the rustic township.

'I had to take care of the guy in the gas station,' he said briefly — and Al and Steve looked at each other.

Steve snapped: 'Y' mean you rubbed him out?'

'Yeah. No other way. He knew who I was. We've gotta fight with the gloves off from here on.'

'Stolen car an' a guy murdered,' Al growled. 'That's swell.'

'Quit beefin', will you, an' give me some co-operation for a change,' Ace growled. 'You got them suitcases safe Al?'

'Yeah — they're right here.'

'Okay. First chance we get, we grab ourselves of some suits an' get a wash — an' we ditch this car. Then we'll try again to get Munro at Scranton. I don't aim to drive straight on, 'cos the cops'll soon know about that garage mechanic, an' the heat'll be on — but good. I'm goin' to double back an' stop at the first place I come to.'

He built up to seventy-five and kept an anxious eye ahead. There was no sign of roadblocks or assembled police cars as yet — but he knew it could happen if he didn't find a side turning before long. Back at the garage, the next customer would find the dead mechanic. The people who'd seen the Buick tearing through the township would tip off the police.

'Over there, to the right,' Al said abruptly. 'Look — a side road. Going over the river.'

Ace nodded, saw traffic approaching, and set his teeth grimly. He whizzed the steering wheel. Tires shrieked. Amidst a blaring of horns and rasping of rubber on stone, he shot across the front of an approaching limousine, missed it by inches, then careered off down the side road in a cloud of dust.

Over the river bridge, along a cart track, through a farmyard, round a corner, down a hill — then Ace was driving like a madman down a vista lined with hedges, a lane which had only enough room for two cars to pass if they inched it at dead slow. He prayed nothing would come from the other way, and drove on.

Nothing did. Ace covered twenty miles flat out before he jammed the skidding car to a halt in a township. He had no idea what name the place had, or even where it was situated on the map. It was small, like the one from which he had come, with a single main street and a huddle of wooden buildings. But one of the buildings was a stores, and it said: 'Tailor' outside.

'All right,' Ace said briefly, turning to look at the trio in the rear seat. 'We ditch the car here and grab ourselves of some clothes. That goes for you too, sister.'

'You hope!' she replied sourly. 'All I can see in that store are men's suits, and I — '

'You'll dress as a man if need be — and like it. Even though I shan't. Stop beefin', an' let's get goin'. And leave the talkin' to me. I'll take those cases, Al. I don't fancy the thought of you perhaps runnin' out if things get hot.'

Ace snapped open the car door and stepped to the wooden sidewalk. He smuggled his Luger into his hand, took the cases from Al, then strode into the tailor's as though he owned it. A glance around assured him it was a kind of general stores as well, with racks of men's and women's clothes standing around on all parts of the floor.

'Morning, sir.' The proprietor, middle-aged, with a tape measure round his neck, came forward. Then he stopped, surveying the rags and tatters in which the four were dressed.

'All right — so we look like somethin' the cat's dragged in,' Ace snapped. 'I want suits for myself and my boys — and a dress for the lady. Hurry it up.'

The man hesitated, his eyes narrowed. 'Say, wait a minute. I guess I just remembered who you are. Ace Monohan. I — '

'You've seen my puss in the papers,' Ace finished for him. 'I figgered you might have. Do as you're told, fella, and — '

Far from doing as he was told, the proprietor made a sudden dive behind his counter. Whether he aimed at snatching up a gun or not, Ace did not wait to see. He made sure by taking out his Luger and firing point blank. The proprietor got the slug in his spine and pitched forward on to his face.

Instantly, Gloria rushed forward and knelt down beside him. There was blank fury in her gray eyes as she looked up again at Ace.

'You killed him!' she cried. 'You trigger-happy bonehead! How much longer do you think you can go around, shooting people up this way?'

'Long as necessary,' Ace told her coldly. 'I said I was fighting with the gloves off, didn't I? Now find yourself a dress while I look for a phone. If anybody comes in. I'll do the talkin'.'

Ace turned and went into the little office. He found the phone and stood watching through the doorway as Al dragged the dead proprietor behind the counter and left him there. Then Munro's voice came over the wire.

'This Seth?' Ace asked. 'Listen. I can't give details, but get that convertible here fast. Pick me up at — wait a minute.' He fished around till he found a bill-head. 'This is Morganville,' he said. 'Step on it, Seth. The heat's killin'.'

He tossed the phone back on its cradle and came back into the store. He was about to say something when he caught sight of Gloria emerging from behind a tall dress rack. She had on a dress that made her look about fourteen. It certainly emphasized which sex she was. Over her right arm, she carried her stained skirt and jacket.

'Very nice,' Ace commented, and she gave him a stony look from her gray eyes.

'What gives?' Al asked, pulling on the cheap jacket of a ready-made. 'Get Seth?'

'Sure thing. The convertible'll be here in twenty minutes.'

'And that stolen Buick's right outside,' Steve pointed out, admiring himself in talkative checks. 'Think that's such a good idea?'

'Mebbe it ain't; but we're right off the beaten track in this dump, ain't we? Cops are only human, anyway; they can't search everywhere in a few minutes.' Ace gave a start as he saw a woman coming to the store's front door.

'Leave it to me,' he said. 'Act like you're trying stuff on.'

He yanked down pants and coat, donned them after he'd ripped off his damaged clothes, and then he strolled into view and went behind the counter. The woman looked at him in surprise.

'I don't seem to know you, young man. Where's Mr. Cavendish?'

'I guess he's out back, ma'am, fixin' the chimney. I've been helping him. That's where all this muck came from on my face — I'm his new assistant.'

The woman studied him; then her eyes strayed to Al, Steve, and Gloria as they fiddled around aimlessly with the clothes stands. Gloria would have spoken right then, only Al had her covered.

Suddenly, the woman said flatly: 'I don't believe you. There's something queer going on in here, and I mean to get at the truth.'

She turned purposefully towards the

door, but Steve intercepted her. His big, ugly face was grinning.

'No you don't, grandma,' he said. 'Get back — go on — move!'

The woman had no choice. Wide-eyed in alarm, she backed towards the nearest clothes stand. Then Al finished the job. Using one of the dresses, he yanked it down over the woman's head, pinning her arms to her sides.

'Take care of her, Ace?' Al asked, glancing across at him.

'No. I don't like rubbin' out women; goes against me better nature. Slug her. Keep her quiet.'

Al nodded, and delivered a bone-splintering punch to the woman's jaw. She dropped soundlessly. Unconcerned, Al rolled her big figure until she, too, was behind the counter.

'S'pose she knows who we are?' he asked Ace.

'Won't make much difference. We'll be outa here and safe before long. I ain't killin' more'n I can help.'

There was silence for a moment, all three men watching the street outside.

Here and there a man or woman passed but none came into the store. Gloria put finger and thumb to her eyes for a moment as though she found the strain of everything too great. Ace looked in her direction and winked at Al. That dress sure was a humdinger. It didn't get any lower than her dimpled knees and, of course, her stockings were missing; the smash had torn them to shreds.

'You'd do better running around with a schoolkid,' Al murmured.

'Ever see a schoolkid with that upholstery?' Ace asked. 'Don't kid yourself.'

He stirred himself at a sudden thought and began collecting his ruined clothes, and those of his boys. He came to Gloria and tried to take her jacket and skirt off her, but she held on to them.

'I've gotta burn the evidence,' he said bluntly. 'So give!'

'Not these,' Gloria retorted, 'They cost plenty of money. When I get clear of you, I'll have them cleaned up.'

Ace looked at her and shrugged, then he investigated the back regions until he found the stove. It didn't take him long to burn the rags up. He came back into the store just as the blue convertible arrived.

'Let's go,' he said abruptly, and bundled the reluctant girl in front of him. She was half flung in the rear cushions, and Steve and Al dropped beside her. Ace, with the suitcases in his hands, dumped himself beside Seth. He was fat, over-fed, immovable — but he knew how to drive. In ten minutes, he had hit a back country road.

'What gives?' Seth asked briefly — so Ace told him.

'I don't like it,' the fat man said. 'It's tough enough for you, grabbing off that Buick — which'll be traced to Morganville in time. It's even worse bringing this girl along. If she's what she says she is, anything can happen. Abduction's a serious business. With two murders thrown in, it'll be hell.'

'Shut up,' Ace said pointedly. 'I know what I'm doing. Y'don't suppose I could leave Gloria to recover an' talk, do you?'

'No reason why not. Only reason you got mixed up with her is because she's a swell-looker. I know your weakness, Ace — and, one day, it'll land you in the chair. Mebbe quite soon.'

Ace said nothing. He sat scowling. Then he looked around him on the deserted countryside and the very distant view of a main road.

'So peaceful, it hurts,' he commented.

'Which is what I don't like,' Steve growled. 'I can't figure why the cops haven't done something in the time they've had. Unless it's like you said, boss, an' they can't be everywhere at once.'

'They aim to let us walk into something,' Ace said. 'That's the real set-up. It's happened before. They don't chase you. Just let you go on running until you can run no more. Won't do 'em any good, though. I guess we can beat a rap like that.'

'How far do you suppose I'm going?' Seth Munro asked. 'I finish at Scranton, remember. My deal with you is to supply this convertible — an' nothin' more. You've added to your overhead already, making me go out to fetch you.'

Ace glanced at him. 'You'll be taken care of. When we get to Scranton, I'll take over.'

'You'd better. This business is much hotter than I was expecting.'

There was silence for a while. Munro swung the big car round bends, up hills, across bridges, and presently hit the high road which led direct to Scranton.

'No other way than this?' Ace snapped.

'Guess not. What are you beefin' about? You look okay — and your girl friend, and the boys.'

'I know. I took that precaution — '

'And we're going to need it,' Al whispered suddenly, leaning over from the back seat. That's a police block just ahead.

He was right. Munro hesitated for the briefest instant, and then kept right on driving. To turn away or reverse would be asking for it. Ace pushed the two hide cases over to the back.

'Put your skirt an' jacket over 'em, sister,' he said.

She remained motionless: then she gasped as Steve brought round his right hand and struck her savagely across the face.

'Do as you're told,' he snapped.

She did, then sat back, wincing and holding her face. Ace gave Steve a look.

'Remind me to step on your kisser some time,' he said sourly. 'If there's any woman-beatin' to be done, I'll do it. Right now,' he added, as the car began to slow down, 'you can leave all the talkin' to me.'

The car stopped. A patrol cop came forward goggles pushed up on his forehead. He surveyed the five in the open car keenly.

'Headed where?' he asked bluntly.

'Scranton,' said the fat man.

'Let's see your license.'

Munro handed it over. A second patrolman walked round the car, looked at the registration number, made a note of it, and then stood looking at Gloria. She half tried to make a signal, and thought better of it as something hard pressed into her side just under the heart.

'What's the idea?' Ace asked, speaking uncommonly well for a change. 'Not usual to be held up on a main highway like this, is it? We're in a hurry.'

'Yeah? Afraid you'll be delayed. What's the rush?'

'Well, no rush,' Ace amended. 'Fishing trip, that's all. But we have my wife's mother to meet.'

Gloria stiffened, and the patrolman's eyes glanced at her.

'I guess you're not doing it very well, Monohan,' the patrolman said. 'You don't suppose your face isn't known to — '

Seth acted. His heavy right fist came up suddenly with blinding impact and struck the patrolman under the jaw. Utterly unprepared, he crashed over backwards and sat in the dust. The second patrolman dived forward. The man beside the roadblock — made up of motorcycles and one police car — hurried to lend assistance.

Seth jammed in the first gear. The engine, still running, burst into violent life. Second gear — third. Seth drove straight at the barrier, sent two motor-cycles flying, then hit the open road beyond. The convertible, tuned to the limit, hurtled forward with ever mounting velocity. It had raced up to sixty before the men left behind had the chance to sort themselves out.

'Only thing to do.' Seth said, breathing hard as he realized Ace was looking at him. 'They spotted you, Ace, and had they gotten away with it, it would have been the finish. I know a quick detour that might throw them.'

Seventy — seventy-five. Seth went all out. From the dim distance came the sound of whining police sirens. The car tires sang on the macadam. Eighty. Seth suddenly swung the wheel, took a highly cambered curve, then swept down a steep hill with such velocity that Gloria closed her eyes. The wind flung back her mass of golden hair.

Pop-eyed, Al and Steve looked about them, ready to leap if things got too tough. Round a bend and up a hill on to the level again. Ahead of them, a level crossing gate was beginning to close. On the up line, a heavy and over-long freight train was clanging its mournful way.

'No!' Ace yelled hoarsely. 'Don't risk it, you damn fool!'

'And be held up till the cops catch up?' Seth hit the floorboard with the accelerator. The closing gates appeared to fly straight at the radiator.

Banging, bumping, the rear of the car taking a piece of gate with it, the convertible shot across the lines, smashed head-on into the gates on the other side, slewed screeching — swung — Then the tires bit stone, and Seth drove on like the devil.

Ace relaxed a little and drew his hand over his forehead, murmuring:

'Nice goin' fella, but you sure had me worried for a minute.'

'From here, we should make it,' Seth said. 'We can hit Scranton without touching the main highway. After that, you can work it out for yourself.'

Ace said nothing more. He was anxiously watching out for more cops, or keeping his ear cocked for a siren, but nothing happened. It seemed clear enough that the police had been stymied when the freight train had gone across their path. It had given Seth just the extra time he needed — with the result that he drew into Scranton without more trouble. It was getting into the afternoon when he did it but, hungry though Ace felt — and his boys and Gloria, too — there could be no let-up.

He paid up Seth, took over the car from him, got the tank filled and thereafter followed out the route he had mapped beforehand. He felt safer doing it this way. When his plans worked smoothly, he was happy; once they went haywire, he fell apart.

Towards three o'clock, he was driving the convertible along a quiet, almost woodland road in the district of Loyalsock, some miles north of Williamsport. Here there was no traffic, no people, no anything — except the roughly-made road, the trees, the sky, and the breeze. It was the kind of place made for a picnic — or a hideout.

'Sooner we can wrap ourselves round some food, the better I'll like it, boss,' Steve complained.

'Stop thinkin' of your stomach,' Ace

growled back at him. 'Anyways, we haven't far to go. You should know that; you've been around here often enough, the both of you.'

He was right in this. Somewhere around here was an old house, which Ace had bought for a song as his funk hole; a deserted old dump where he could go to cover until the heat was off. It was half hidden in woodland and almost falling apart, but some of it was still habitable. Probably take the police the rest of their lives to locate it.

By four o'clock, Ace had discovered it, at the end of a short, winding lane. He drew the car up outside rusty gates, almost falling off their hinges, and looked up the weed-covered drive. The house was visible amidst the thickly clustered trees.

'Welcome home,' he said dryly. 'Get out, Al, and open up the gates.'

Al obeyed. When he had dragged them apart, Ace drove up to the front porch and stopped the car. Stiffly he clambered out and whipped open the back door.

'Out you get, sister,' he said, and

yanked the two hide cases from where they still lay under her coat and skirt.

Gloria obeyed. Ace watched her move, and it made him forget his troubles for the moment.

'I don't like being stared at,' she said bitterly, as Ace found a key on his chain.

'You'll get used to it, kid,' he grinned and strode up to the porch way. He had the door open in a moment and it swung on to dust, gloom, and the smell of not-lived-in.

'After you, sweetheart,' Ace said, giving the girl a nudge.

He followed her in, with Steve and Al coming up behind. They all crossed the ancient hall and came into a wide living room. It had a table, a few chairs, a divan — and that was all. No electric lights, or anything civilized. Only an unlighted oil lamp on the table, where a solitary ray of sunlight hit it. There were echoes, dusty floorboards, grimy windows, and age. It made Gloria shiver. She came to a stop by the fireplace — huge and draughty — and looked at the oaken beams of the ceiling. Here and there, enormous hooks had been driven in the beams, probably from the time when lanterns had hung there. The ceiling itself went up in diagonal panels, instead of lying flat.

'All the comforts of home,' Ace said, rubbing his hands. 'I sure got the right idea when I picked this dump for a hideout.'

'What do we live on?' Gloria asked coldly. 'Air?'

'No — there's food an' drink in the kitchen, and an oil stove for cookin'. I reckon that's where you come into it.'

'You think!'

'I know. You'll earn your keep here, sister, believe me. Since I've had to bring you along for my own protection. I'm going to make use of you, too. You'll find we've got everything here. All been planned ahead of time. Even beds upstairs, though I reckon we're one short, 'cos I hadn't figured you'd be comin'.'

Gloria folded her arms and waited, half sitting on the table top.

'I'll show you where we cook,' Steve said. 'First thing we do is eat and drink. Follow me.'

'Al can do that,' Ace said. 'Better follow him, kid.'

Gloria slid from the table and stood up. Ace stood admiring the delectable roundness of her curves as she walked from the room. That size-too-small dress was a masterpiece. Then he turned slowly to look at Steve. Steve was frowning, puzzled.

'Why couldn't I show her the kitchen, boss? What gives?'

Ace moved over to him, considered — and then he lashed up his right in a hammer blow. Steve absorbed it on the jaw and crashed backwards against the table, clutching at it for support.

'That's for the dame,' Ace explained, jerking his cuffs straight. 'Don't ever hit her again, or I'll kill you. Get it?'

Steve straightened up sullenly and said nothing. He knew that, when Ace talked like that, he meant it.

'That's all,' Ace added. 'Go give a hand to get the food.'

3

The man with the wide shoulders stepped in swiftly between the revolving doors of the 'Silver Slipper', one of the most prosperous clip joints on the East Side. He hurried past the men slapping mops and dusting tables preparatory to the evening's round of gypping then he went round the dried palms, along a softly carpeted corridor, and stopped at a walnut door. He knocked once, and opened the door as an easy voice bade him step in.

Jonathan 'Fingers' Baxter was at his desk. He owned the 'Silver Slipper' and several other clip joints as well. He knew just how to stay on the right side of the DA.; he knew just how to thumb his nose at the police and smile at the same time. 'Fingers' was in fact, a very smooth guy. Not yet thirty-six, he knew exactly what life added up to. An education of sorts and slick good looks helped him whenever he felt himself slipping.

'Seen this?' asked the man with the wide shoulders, and flung down the first edition of the evening paper.

'Fingers' set aside the accounts he was studying and picked up the newspaper. He swiveled his chair round so the sunlight glancing over the top of the neighboring skyscrapers caught the deep waves in his blond hair and made his blue eyes seem transparent. He was very nearly handsome — except for a mouth like a steel trap.

'Filanti's joint, eh?' he asked, grinning. 'Nearly two hundred grand's worth cleaned up. Nice work — so what?' he finished, and looked over his shoulder.

'I got an idea,' said the man with the wide shoulders. 'The cops're either slippin', or else whoever did this job is mighty smart. Fact remains, nobody's bin caught. And that means that somewheres around, there must be all that ice waitin', and the guys responsible won't move till the heat's off.'

'Go right on talking,' 'Fingers' invited, thinking.

'According to the report, the cops got

themselves ditched — an' two guys have been bumped off, an' a woman knocked. It also looks as though there was five guys on the job at first, an' then it dropped to three, with a dame thrown in. But there ain't no description of any of 'em.'

'Fingers' lit a cigarette. 'Very often isn't. The cops don't always play the game our way by describing exactly who they are looking for. Wouldn't be smart on their part. Where's all this leading, Mugsy?'

Mugsy said: 'I'm wonderin' if mebbe it was Ace Monohan who pulled this job. Sure wasn't an amatoor — an' if Ace got ambitious, it's just the sorta snatch he'd work out. Two hundred grand ain't hay. He musta worked on it for a long time — if it was him. Only bumpings-off don't sound like him. He's usually very careful.'

'Maybe he can't be careful any more,' 'Fingers' said, and sat considering, hard lights in his eyes.

'You may be right,' he said, after a moment. 'An' if there's one thing in this life I aim to do, it's blot out Ace — or, failing that, take from him whatever he likes best. There never was enough room for both of us.'

Mugsy nodded, but kept quiet. The bitter enmity between Ace and 'Fingers' was common knowledge in the quarters where it counted. Mugsy himself had more than once fallen foul of Ace's boys and taken a beating in consequence. He'd like to see Ace fry, or else get sprung into the lap of the police. Otherwise, he would not have given himself the unaccustomed job of thinking so hard.

'Could be,' 'Fingers' agreed, at length. 'If it was Ace, I'll shift everythin' to find him — an' even if it isn't, I don't see all that ice lying on one side, when a bit of work on our part might unearth it. What we want to find out is if it was Ace. If so, there's plenty of contacts we can make to find out just where Ace has ducked to.'

'Yeah — but how'd we find out if it was him?'

'Shouldn't be difficult. The police won't tell us,' 'Fingers' grinned, 'so the only thing for it is to ask one of the staff at Filanti's what the hold-up men looked like. They're probably sworn to secrecy by the police, but there's nothing like gentle persuasion to soften 'em up.'

'I don't like it, 'Fingers',' Mugsy said uneasily. 'If I take some of the boys an' go walkin' into Filanti's for information, I might even run into the cops. They've probably got the place cased.'

'Fingers' aimed him a look. 'Use that thing on your shoulders for other things than holding a hat,' he said. 'You don't go into Filanti's, you dope; you wait till the staff comes out. Then follow the most likely one, an' get all the description you can.'

'Uh-huh. An' what happens then? Whoever we get will tell the cops that the information's been handed on, and that may lead us straight into Captain McArdel's office.'

'You gettin' soft-hearted?' 'Fingers' asked, in surprise. 'I thought you knew by now never to let anybody talk if they can be stopped. Just get rid of the informer — that's all. Now get going — and do the job yourself. The staff from Filanti's should leave around six.'

Mugsy went — and 'Fingers' returned

to his accounts. He always remained in his office when anything important went on elsewhere; surest way of providing an airtight alibi. Nobody knew better than he how much the police could be stymied without exactly the right kind of evidence.

From the 'Silver Slipper', Mugsy drifted across town until he reached Filanti's. He took up a position on the opposite side of the busy street and studied the place for a while. Then he crossed over and, through the windows, got a view of the salon's interior whilst apparently idly surveying the stuff on show. He noticed there were three young women and one man comprising the staff. The women were pretty good-lookers, but two of them were beyond the interesting age. The third one was the kind who might talk easily, if coaxed the right way. The man was hard-looking and might not talk, anyway.

Mugsy had made up his mind by the time he crossed over the street again. Thereafter, he killed time as best he could until, around six, the satin drapes were drawn over the salon windows and the man came out to lock the steel guards across them. Mugsy grinned as he saw, and spat casually.

He saw the three women leave, each going their separate ways. Two of them he ignored, the third he began to tail from the other side of the street, then, at a convenient break in the traffic, he crossed over and saw her enter a subway station. He followed, sat near her, and got out when she did.

When she came to the surface, her course took her first along busy streets, shimmering with the heat of June evening sunlight; then, by degrees, she got away from the busy regions into quieter short cuts which took her in the general direction of apartment houses.

When she cut through a short alleyway, Mugsy saw his chance. Either side of the alley were tall, windowless walls. Nobody could overlook. The chances of anybody else coming this way were remote. The girl was aware of him coming, for she heard his quick footfalls. Surprised, she paused for a moment, and glanced over her shoulder. Evidently scenting danger, she broke into a run but, in ten strides, Mugsy had overtaken her and grabbed her arm. She looked down at the automatic he pressed into her side.

'What — what do you want?' she asked hoarsely, clinging to her handbag. 'If — if it's money, I haven't above ten dollars.'

'Keep it, sweetheart. All I want from you is a few nice words, but it may not be safe to get 'em right here, baby.' He looked about him swiftly, noted the enormous disused granary nearby, and nodded to it. 'Get in there,' he ordered.

'But I haven't done anything,' the girl protested. 'Look, mister, I — '

'Shut up, and move. This isn't candy I'm sticking in your ribs. Hurry it up.'

Helplessly, the salesgirl moved. Directed by Mugsy, she crossed the granary's deserted yard and then entered the open, abandoned ground floor of the place. It was full of dust and broken glass from shattered windows. She came to a stop in the choking gloom, her heart hammering. Mugsy loomed in front of her.

'This mornin', your joint was stuck up,'

he said. 'Who pulled that job? You musta seen them.'

'I — I can't tell you.' The girl had very wide blue eyes, plain scared. 'The police said we mustn't tell anybody.'

'Yeah? Why not?'

'I don't know. Just orders from Captain McArdel.'

'I mighta known,' Mugsy sneered. 'Just forget the Captain, an' tell me what you know, before I hafta beat it outa you.'

'The man who talked to me and told me to keep quiet was Ace Monohan,' the girl said, in a sudden rush.

'Sure?'

'He said so. He had a flat first finger, I noticed — if that means anything.'

'That's Ace,' Mugsy reflected. 'That's all I wanted to know.'

The girl began to breathe more freely. 'You mean I can go now? That's all you wanted of me?'

Mugsy looked at her, then around him. Her frightened eyes followed him. He was powerful, and had an automatic trained on her. She just dare not move or cry out. Her legs began to shake so much they'd hardly keep her up.

'The minute you're away from here, you'll talk,' Mugsy said grimly, glancing back at her as he surveyed the emptiness. 'You'll go straight to homicide and tell McArdel that you've had to tell me. That won't be good.'

'I won't! I swear I won't! You've got to let me go!'

The girl swung and made a dash for it. She only moved a few yards, then Mugsy caught her shoulder and held on it, dragging her to a standstill.

'I can't put a slug in you, because of the noise,' he said briefly. 'Might bring somebody. But I reckon there's other ways of keepin' you quiet. If it were dark, I'd sling you in the river.'

The salesgirl knew, in that moment, that the finger was on her. She lashed and struggled savagely as the thug seized hold of her more tightly, his big hand now smothering her screams. She fought wildly, in a hopeless chaos of dust and silence, cut off from those not far away, who would have saved her.

Her gay kerchief was suddenly ripped

from her throat and tied tight across her mouth so her teeth bit into it. The belt from her frock pinned her wrists behind her. Her eyes glazed with fright, she lay squirming in the dirt and refuse, thrashing her feet savagely and uselessly as Mugsy stood looking down at her. He put his gun away.

'Sorry, kid, that you've got to pass out,' he said, 'but I guess orders are all I'm concerned about.'

Stooping, he picked up her struggling form in his powerful arms and carried her across to where a thick rope from the upper loft of the granary hung down. He moved it methodically and then slipped it over the girl's neck. There was something about the way she looked at him at that moment that made him turn away. He'd seen a puppy look at him like that once.

When he had made the rope fast to its staple in the wall, he looked back once, then picked up the girl's handbag and put it under his coat. The gloom of the great place was deeper now, and the silence complete, save for the faint creak of a rope swinging back and forth, back and forth . . .

But Mugsy had a short memory. He was himself again by the time he got back to the 'Silver Slipper'. Customers were arriving in the bright lights. Still with the girl's bag hidden, he made his way to 'Fingers'' office. He was in his tuxedo polishing his nails, as Mugsy entered.

'Well?' he asked briefly.

'It's Ace,' Mugsy said, and tossed down the handbag on the desk. 'One of the salesgirls told me — then I shut her up like you said.'

'How?'

'Necktie.'

'Hmmm,' 'Fingers' said, and examined his nails.

Mugsy opened the handbag and tipped out the contents on the blotter. Compact, handkerchief, small penknife, a ticket for a dance, small change, visiting card. He looked at the name on the bag behind the little oblong celluloid window.

'Betty Hopson,' he said. 'That was her monicker.'

'I hope, for your sake, Mugsy, that you

didn't leave anything behind,' 'Fingers' said, eyeing him. 'It'll be just too bad if you did. Remember, you rubbed her out; I didn't.'

Mugsy grinned. 'Ain't the first one I rubbed out, and I'm still here.'

'Fingers' looked at the assortment on the desk, then motioned his immaculate right hand.

'Burn this stuff — every trace of it. Then take the boys and find out where Ace might be likely to have gone to cover. I've got to find him. Work as fast as you can, and don't pull your punches. I'm not having Ace lying around with all that stuff and getting away with it. Soon as you've got something, tell me about it. Now blow.'

Mugsy went, taking the handbag and its contents with him, under his coat.

★   ★   ★

Ace sat back in his chair at the table and held out his jeweled cigarette case.

'No, thanks,' Gloria said, seated next to him, with folded arms.

Ace looked at her in the wavering glow of the oil lamp. The darkness was setting in. Heavy drapes had been drawn over the windows. Around the table, with its assortment of crockery and greasy dishes, Al and Steve sat watching their boss, and then the girl, narrowly. All of them had eaten and finished the coffee. It seemed like a moment to examine the situation so far.

'I don't like your attitude, sister,' Ace said finally, blowing smoke through his nostrils. 'Give me a bit of co-operation, can't you?'

'How?' Her gray eyes pinned him. She had an insolence in her pretty face which galled him. 'Want me to throw my arms round your neck, or something?'

'It's an idea. Mebbe you will, before I'm through with you. What's wrong with me, anyways? I'm not so bad-looking. I'm worth plenty of greenbacks — an' even more so when the stuff I just took is handed over.'

'To whom?' Gloria questioned.

'A guy from Harrisburg. I'll be contacting him when the heat's off.'

The girl considered him, then she shook her blonde head and sighed.

'You just don't see anything wrong in what you've done, do you?'

'There ain't nothin' wrong in it. If you gyp anybody legally, it's called speculation. If it's a hold-up, it's robbery. There ain't no difference.'

'There is when you throw murder in, too.'

Ace said bitterly. 'It ain't always possible to play the game the way one would like it. I've got my interests to look after, an' I'm not takin' any chances on any guy talkin'.'

Gloria got to her feet and considered Ace with bleak eyes.

'You're a parasite,' she said. 'A dirty, cheap parasite. The kind who make it tough for decent people to live straight.'

Ace had the corners of his mouth dragged down. The light was casting sideways on to Gloria, throwing the swelling roundness of her breasts and the arch of her neck into relief.

'Don't like it, do you?' she asked. 'First time anybody ever told you what a tinhorn you are, isn't it?'

'I can take it, kid — from you.'

'If she said it to me, I'd kick her teeth out,' Steve muttered.

'Scum, the lot of you,' Gloria said, and threw back her blonde head. 'Three men — one woman. I'm right at your mercy, and you know it; but that doesn't stop me saying what I think. And you'll never get away with this, either. The police aren't such fools as you think. What's more, I'll help them if I can. Once they get you, Ace, you'll fry. And these boys of yours will get long sentences.'

Ace got slowly on his feet. His shortness made him only as tall as the girl herself. She remained looking at him, hands at her sides, frozen contempt in her smoke-gray eyes.

'Any funny business from you, sister, an' I'll forget you're a dame, an' let you have it,' he said. 'Anyway, what are you beefin' about? Nobody's hurt you, have they — 'cept Steve, an' I've already taken care of him for that slap in the kisser he gave you.'

'Nice of you,' Gloria answered. 'I don't

want your protection, Ace. I'd sooner make friends with a cobra. Now, where do I sleep? I'm tired.'

'There's a divan there,' Ace said, nodding. 'Make do with that. Al, get some blankets from upstairs.'

'While you heels have beds, you mean?' Gloria demanded sarcastically.

'Ain't that. You could have had a bed, but you might escape. I'm keepin' an eye on you — down here. An' when I'm not doin' it, Al or Steve will be. If you want your shut-eye, the divan's all you're gettin'.'

Gloria shrugged. 'Maybe I'm not sleepy,' she said, but she went over to the divan, nevertheless, and lay down upon it, stretching herself lazily, putting her hands behind her head. Ace stood looking at her, lithe and smoothly rounded. He clenched his fists and took a half step towards her; then he turned back as Steve spoke, in his slow, brutal voice:

'How long d'you reckon we stop here, boss? It ain't no fun, no matter how you look at it.'

'We stay here until it's safe to move

— an' stop askin' questions.'

'Y'mean stop interruptin' you lookin' at the dame,' Steve corrected. 'Not that I blame you,' he added, as he surveyed her.

She took no notice. She still lay looking at the ceiling, her hands supporting her head. Ace gave her another glance, and then went over to the radio. He switched it on to short wave and listened. Nothing very interesting. Just news flashes. Finally, he switched it off again.

'Like I said — so peaceful it hurts,' he commented. 'I guess the cops are tryin' to pull somethin'. They can't be so dumb they don't know about a stolen Buick, a jumped police block, a snatch, an two rubbings-out?'

'Won't be easy for them to find us here,' Al pointed out, picking his teeth with a match sliver.

'No — I guess it won't.'

Silence. Ace stood thinking. Gloria slanted her eyes and looked at him. After a while, he aroused himself again and motioned.

'You mugs had better grab some

shut-eye, and then take over from me later on. I'm staying here. Keep an eye on the dame.'

'Won't be difficult,' Steve said, getting up.

'You shut up, before I smear you on the wall.'

Steve shrugged and ambled out. Al followed him after a moment, and the door closed. Presently there were sounds overhead as the two men went to their rooms.

'It's time,' Ace said, looking down at the girl from beside the table, 'for you and me to get things straight, sister.'

'The name's Vane,' Gloria said, without looking at him. 'Gloria Vane to my friends. Miss Vane to a tramp like you.'

Suddenly, Ace whirled. He dived straight at the girl, caught her shoulders in his big hands, and shook her violently.

'D'you think you can just lie there an' spit at me?' he demanded. 'Do you?'

She did not answer, but the look in her eyes infuriated him all the more. Transferring his hands to her arms, he dragged her up from the sofa and held her tightly against him. She was warm and supple in his steel embrace for a moment, every curve and line pressing into him.

'You dirty great beast,' she whispered, and with unexpected violence, her right hand lashed up and hit him across the eyes.

Dazed, he released her — so suddenly, she stumbled backwards, and fell heavily against the divan. Ace blinked, his eyes watering.

'Keep away from me,' she whispered, her eyes glinting amidst her tumbled hair. 'Don't touch me, or I'll kick your — '

Ace took no notice. Stooping, he dodged the kick she aimed at him. She made to scramble away, but he swung round and loomed in front of her. His hands under her armpits, he heaved her up in front of him, and stood looking into her flushed, angry face. For some reason, she didn't budge in his grip. A thought was drifting in her mind. As she had lain on the floor, she had noticed something — a hard bulge in Ace's hip-pocket. His automatic . . . that was the one key out of this place.

'Gettin' sensible?' Ace asked grimly.

She said nothing. His hands pushing up under her arms stopped her reaching down as low as his hip-pocket. She raised her hands and took hold of his strong wrists, forcing his grip away from her. She breathed hard and tossed the fallen hair out of her eyes.

'All right, Ace, you win,' she said quietly. 'I ought to have known, with a man like you. I just don't stand a chance.'

He looked at her and frowned. She sank down on the divan and pinned back her disordered hair. The dress had split at one shoulder, leaving a zig-zag of stitches over her white flesh.

'I don't get it,' Ace said bluntly, and spat the stump of his cigarette from the corner of his mouth, heeling it on the floor behind him.

'Don't get what?' Gloria looked up at him and spread her hands. 'I'm trying to tell you I'm sorry for the things I said. You may not be every girl's idea of a hero, but you certainly behave like a man — and that's something. I thought you were just aiming to stand around and spit vitriol at me.'

Ace sat down beside her, caught her shoulder, and looked at her flushed face.

'Y'mean — no hard feelings?'

She smiled. It cost her an effort, but she smiled just the same. Relaxing back on to the divan, she looked at him intently.

'You're different from most men I have ever met' she said 'In my business they're mostly lens-lizards. They may look tough while they're paid for it. Outside that, they aren't hardly worth knowing — the ones I've met up with, anyway. You're different. You take things as you find them — women included.'

'Woman,' he corrected. 'Only one, as far as I'm concerned. I wouldn't have taken the risk of bringing you along with me otherwise.'

Gloria did not say anything. Ace leaned forward, his hands gripping the tops of her arms and his lips crushing on to hers. She closed her eyes and felt down with her hand. She had got as near as the bulge in his hip-pocket when he straightened up again.

69

'No reason why you an' me can't relax together for a while,' he said, taking his cigarette case from his shirt pocket. 'Have one this time?'

She accepted. He could not kiss her whilst she had a weed in her mouth. He lit the cigarette for her, then tossed the case on the nearby table. To her consternation, the automatic followed it.

'That's better,' he said, grinning, putting an arm about her shoulders. 'Now it's time we got to know one another better, ain't it?'

4

Captain Duncan McArdel of New York's Homicide Division, sixth precinct, sat thinking. It was the morning following the raid on Filanti's salon. The big Scotsman with an American birthright was amongst the most hated of men — as far as law-breakers were concerned. To those intimate with him, he was renowned for his unorthodox methods and relentless persistency.

'So that's as far as we've got, boys,' he said finally, and the two plainclothes men standing beside the big desk nodded.

'We've got everything, chief, except where he is,' one of them said.

McArdel nodded. He was heavy-limbed, fortyish, with hair turning prematurely gray. He had a face so square, a cartoonist might have created it.

'First Filanti's,' he said. 'Then a smash, and three men found dead. A red car, identified as belonging to one Gloria

Vane, a movie actress, who has since disappeared from sight.'

'That's right,' the first man agreed. 'I've tried to get a line on her from Hollywood, but nothing seems to register. She's not in the big money; just a young character actress, with plenty of ability, but not much prospects. No relatives, apparently. She was in rooms in Hollywood, and the last her landlady heard of her was three weeks ago, when she — the girl, I mean — said she was coming to New York here to talk to the agent who handles her.'

'Where did all this news come from?' McArdel demanded keenly.

'I tried the various companies until I got the one who'd last employed her, then I got the dope from their casting office.'

'And what about her agent here — does he know anything at all?'

'No. He wasn't even aware that the girl was coming to talk things over with him.'

McArdel considered. 'Which means nobody will be looking for the girl — or, at least, nobody will be able to help me with information. We know she's with Ace because the folks who saw that getaway in

Morganville report a blonde piece was in the Buick.' He sifted the reports. 'A pretty set-up, in fact. Her car wrecked; three dead men in Ace's sedan. A stolen Buick. A girl snatched, two men murdered and a woman trussed up, a fat guy in Scranton who won't talk, and a police block jumped. Ace is sure going the limit, and he seems to have dropped neatly out of sight.'

'His trail seems to end at Scranton, chief,' said the second man. 'The fat man knows all the answers, I think, but he's keeping quiet. Can't say if he knows where Ace is, though.'

'So what do we do?' McArdel got up from his swivel chair and began pacing the office slowly. He stopped after a while and looked at the big wall map; then he said: 'From Scranton, Ace could go north, south, east or west, and vanish into countryside in each direction. Naturally, he'd got it all planned.'

'Why didn't somebody get on his tail?' one of the men demanded. 'According to report, the fat man said he was going to Scranton. I can't figure why the boys in that road block didn't tell 'em at Scranton to be or the look-out.'

'They did,' McArdel said dryly. 'But Scranton isn't a fishing village remember. It's the hell of a big place — and it's plain this fat guy knows the layout like the back of his hand. He got into the city by side routes. It would have taken every copper in the place to watch all the routes leading into it — so the fat guy got away with it, and Ace must have driven out again by a route which wasn't covered. Fact remains he got clear, and where he is right now, I don't know.'

'Time we started looking, then,' said the first man.

'I guess so,' McArdel agreed. 'Find out all you can, boys, making Scranton your base. Take Matthews and Lloyd with you, and arrange your own reliefs. Call me back the minute you find out something.'

The two men nodded and left the office, just as Sergeant Clayton came in. He had a page of his scratchpad in his hand.

'Riley just rang in, chief,' he said. 'There's a woman been hanged in

Bailey's granary — a deserted joint over near the river.'

'Go and take a look at it,' McArdel growled. 'I've too much on my mind with this Monohan business right now to — '

'The girl's Betty Hopson, chief,' the sergeant broke in. 'She has a staff identity card on a ribbon round her neck. Seems she was head saleswoman at Filanti's before somebody took care of her.'

'Filanti's?' McArdel looked up sharply. 'Say, that really is interesting. What's this about an identity card you mention?'

'Same as many big jewelry firms do. They give their important employees an identity card to keep on them, in case some time when they're transporting valuables, something happens to 'em. Evidently, this girl wore hers like a locket. Good job she did. Saves us some trouble. No other clues. The card must have escaped whoever killed her.'

'I'll take a look right now,' McArdel said quickly. 'How about the boys? Finger-prints, photographers, surgeon, and the rest of it?'

'On their way, chief. I tipped them off.'

'Okay. You'd better come with me.'

They left the precinct headquarters together and, the sergeant driving, had reached the granary ten minutes later. The boys were already there, taking photographs, the fingerprint men had left, having nothing to work on. The police surgeon was just packing up his bags.

'Strangulation,' he said briefly, as McArdel eyed him. 'That rope up there — ' He nodded to it where it hung slashed, the body now on its back beneath it. 'Whoever killed this poor kid tied her hands with her own dress belt and then strung her up. I guess business gets filthier every day, Mac.'

'Guess it does.' McArdel muttered, moving forward.

'I'll send in my report,' the medico threw back over his shoulder.

McArdel wasn't listening. His eyes were fixed on the body of Betty Hopson. Her face was dead white now, and the eyes closed. The staring evidence of her agonizing death had gone.

'Unlikely Ace did this,' McArdel said at length.

'Why is it?' The sergeant seemed surprised. 'He was the only one — apart from his boys, I mean — mixed up in the Filanti job. I should think he'd be just the one to take care of this dame. Or more likely one of his boys did. Probably she knew too much.'

'No, you're wrong. Each one of the staff knew Ace's identity; they told us that much themselves. We've had no reports of any of the others being rubbed out, so that doesn't seem like the answer. It was more likely somebody who wanted to know the identity of the hold-up men, and this girl happened to be singled out for attention. Mebbe because she was the giving kind; I noticed that when I talked to her at the salon.'

'Which means she met her death 'cos you swore them and the press to secrecy. I don't get that bit, chief. Seemed queer.'

McArdel moved irritably. 'There's no use telling a crook you know his identity and that he did it; that way, he knows you're wise to him. If he isn't sure you have his number, he's liable to take risks. That was my reason. I didn't think it'd cause this sort of thing.'

'If it wasn't some of Ace's work, who else?'

'As a long shot — 'Fingers' Baxter,' McArdel said grimly. 'He and Ace have been enemies for years. Can you imagine how 'Fingers' would feel at realizing all that stuff had been grabbed off and he hadn't even had a smell of it? Because no names were given, he would not know it was Ace. In any case, it wouldn't matter who it was so long as he could find out who was at the back of it and try and get a cut for himself — I think,' McArdel finished, 'that 'Fingers' is due for an interview very soon.'

'Okay. Do I rope him in to the office?'

'No. I'll go and see him myself. I've no specific charge for bringing him in for questioning — as he'd be quick to tell me. I'll see what I can dig up. You stay here until the boys have finished and the ambulance has cleaned up this body. Fix things up with the Coroner. I'll see you later.'

'Walking?'

'Uh-huh,' McArdel assented. 'It's not

so far to the 'Silver Slipper'.'

He was there in fifteen minutes, to discover that 'Fingers' had just arrived. He was in the act of taking off his lemon-colored gloves as McArdel inserted himself into the office.

'Well?' 'Fingers' looked at him and grinned. 'An early caller — and none the more welcome for that. Just what gives Captain?'

'I'd like a word with you, 'Fingers'.'

'You would, huh? What about? You've nothing on me, and you can't prove I don't run my joints on the up-and-up.'

'Fingers' settled himself at the desk, his blue eyes as wide as a baby's, and a friendly grin on his steel-trap mouth.

McArdel sat on the edge of the desk. 'I'm not interested in your joints right now, 'Fingers'. Ever hear of a girl by the name of Betty Hopson?'

'Should I have?' 'Fingers' examined his nails pensively.

'I think you should. She was strung up in a granary because she probably knew too much about the Filanti robbery.'

'Why pick on me?' 'Fingers' snapped. 'I

didn't pull the Filanti job, and you know darned well I didn't.'

'Mebbe, but that doesn't stop you being interested in it. Two hundred thousand bucks' worth of stuff might be worth your attention if you could find out who took it, and where that person is. Any of the staff from Filanti's could be made to talk, and my guess is that one of them was made to — Betty Hopson.'

'Look, Captain, I've the constitutional right to object to this,' 'Fingers' looked up malevolently. 'You coming right in here and accusing me of wiping out this dame.'

'Correct,' McArdel agreed grimly. 'And don't hand me that line about constitutional rights, either. It don't sound good from a killer who sits in a swivel chair and gets other mugs to do the rubbing out. You and I understand each other, 'Fingers', so we can talk off the record. Words never got anybody into court. You're in the clear only because you have the brains to smother all evidence that might point to you. The first mistake you make, I'll bounce you good and hard.'

'All right; so we understand each other.' 'Fingers' said sourly. 'Now blow. I don't like the smell of a copper.'

McArdel got up from the desk and said slowly: 'That Mugsy's slipping, 'Fingers'. He shouldn't leave so many clues around after pulling a job like that one with Betty Hopson.'

'Fingers' gave the slightest of starts and looked up. It was enough for McArdel. He gave a brief nod then turned and left the office. 'Fingers' sat thinking for a moment; then he savagely jabbed the bell push on his desk. After a moment or two, a waiter looked in, holding his mop in one hand.

'Want something, boss?'

'I want Mugsy. Is he anywhere around?'

'I ain't seen him, boss. He went out last evening and told me he didn't know when he'd be back.'

'Fingers' nodded and jerked his head. The waiter went, and the door closed. For the moment, 'Fingers' had overlooked the fact that he had detailed Mugsy to try and find out where Ace had gone to cover.

'The big, blundering ape,' 'Fingers' muttered, and snatched a cigarette from the box on the table before him. 'If he's slipped up as much as McArdel seems to think, this can get tough. I'll half kill the guy when I see him.'

When he did see him, it was mid-morning. Mugsy came lounging in with a grin on his square, brutal face. He lost it when he saw the icy glint in his boss's eyes.

'What did you leave around for the cops to find after you rubbed out Betty Hopson?' 'Fingers' demanded.

'Me?' Mugsy thought for a moment. 'I didn't leave anything. I took good care not to.'

'You must have done something, otherwise how does McArdel know the girl's name is Betty Hopson, and that you bumped her off?'

'It just — ain't possible,' Mugsy declared, staring.

'You'll be telling me next I imagined it when he stepped into the office here and grilled me for a few minutes. He's on to you, Mugsy, though I don't know right now how far he intends going.'

'I still say there ain't nothin' he can pin on me,' the thug retorted. 'I'm particular when I take care of anybody I hafta be.'

'See what develops,' 'Fingers' muttered. 'Anyway, what are you doing here? Thought I told you to find out where Ace has ducked to?'

'I did find out, even if I did have to use some persuasion here and there.' Mugsy sat on the desk edge and cuffed up his hat on to his forehead. 'I got hold of a guy who delivered some furniture for Ace — '

'Furniture?' 'Fingers' stared in surprise.

'Yeah. He drove it out on a truck to a place two miles north of Loyalsock, Penn. An old house. or something, way off the beaten track. There was beds and tables and chairs: all the stuff you might need for a happy home. Since he did it for Ace, I guess Ace musta been thinkin' of retirin' at the time.'

'Yeah — retiring with two hundred smackers in rocks and ice,' 'Fingers' mused. 'What did it cost you to find out this much?'

Mugsy grinned. 'Didn't cost me any-thing. Cost the guy who told me quite a lot. I plugged him.'

'You damned trigger-happy gorilla!' 'Fingers' jumped to his feet. 'If you keep on rubbing out people this way, you — '

'I *didn't* rub him out, boss — just made him so's he'll limp for a bit. I had to get out safely. He can't do nothing, even though he knows who I am. Can't do anything with you running things. Not that he'll try to be smart, I don't suppose. All he did was deliver furniture and get paid for it.'

'He might warn Ace that we're trying to find him, an' that'd get him on the move.'

Mugsy said nothing. He hadn't thought of that.

'But Ace can't move far.' 'Fingers' went on, thinking. 'Is two miles north of Loyalsock the best you can do?'

'I guess so. Exact place doesn't seem to have a name. We'll hafta search for ourselves.'

'We will — tonight,' 'Fingers' decided. 'Rustle up the boys during the day, get yourselves some hardware, and we'll see what we can do. Now get out of here. I have work to do.'

'You mean you're coming yourself tonight, boss? You don't often step out when we — '

'Shut up. You don't suppose I'm trusting you gorillas with all that stuff, do you? 'Sides, Ace and me have a score to settle.'

Mugsy left the office. About the same time, Captain McArdel was in his own headquarters, looking through the various reports that had been sent in, all of them relating to Betty Hopson's murder.

'We don't know it was Mugsy, even though you've guessed at it, chief,' the sergeant said. 'You say you told that to 'Fingers' straight out. Why?'

'To watch his reaction. I know 'Fingers' as well as I know myself, and his expression quite satisfied me. It was Mugsy who killed Betty Hopson. That big ape does all 'Fingers'' dirty work, but I've no proof.'

'That's what has me bothered. Why

mention it when you can't do anything about it?'

McArdel sat back in his chair. 'Listen, the one thing 'Fingers' wants is to find Ace — and he can do it far better than we can, because he can move freely in the underworld dives, whereas we can't, because nobody there will spill anything to a cop. If we sit back, I figure that 'Fingers' will do our work for us. He'll find out where Ace is hiding with that jewelry, even if it kills him. So, since I'm certain Mugsy found out all the information he wanted from Betty Hopson our next job is to keep tabs on 'Fingers' and see if it leads us somewhere. I've already got three men on the lookout.'

The sergeant grinned. 'Nice work, chief, though I say it. But isn't Mugsy — and 'Fingers', too — going to think things when you don't rope Mugsy in for questioning about Betty Hopson?'

'Probably.' McArdel said. 'But the thing to remember is that 'Fingers's' main concern at the moment is getting at Ace. Other matters won't bother him much. I'm hoping, if he leads us to Ace, that I may be able to nail not only Ace, but 'Fingers' as well, and with those two boys out of the way, the town'll be a darned sight cleaner. Mugsy, we can take care of later.'

The sergeant nodded and left it at that.

★ ★ ★

Ace was beginning to fret. Not because there were signs of danger, but because there were not. It was noon now, and he had spent the morning pacing around the vast, rambling house and smoking cigarettes. At the table — the crockery from the rough breakfast pushed in a heap on the rickety sideboard — Al and Steve sat playing an interminable crap game.

'Good job there ain't no carpet down,' Steve commented, after a while.

'All right for you,' Ace growled at him, halting by the table. 'I've the thinking to do. You mugs have only to take orders, fill your bellies, or play around with a dame. Different for me. I got all the responsibility.'

'And the pickings,' Steve said, raising

his eyes for a moment. 'Which reminds me, boss — how do we cut this deal?'

'Same as we always do. Twenty-five per cent each for you two; fifty per cent for me.'

'Pickings,' Steve said, 'is right.'

Ace took his Luger from his hip pocket. He had put it back there when he had finished his hour's relaxation with Gloria.

'Want to argue about it?' he demanded.

'Nope.' Steve gave a shrug. 'Not while you're on that end of the hardware.'

Steve went on playing his hand, unmoved. Al reflected and glanced towards the closed door that led to the second ground floor of the house.

'Sure that dame's safe in there?' he asked. 'If she gets outa here and starts talking, it'll be the finish.'

'Suppose you let me worry about her?' Ace put his gun back in his pocket. 'She an' me understand each other now.'

'That ain't no reason to gamble with our safety,' Al pointed out. 'I wouldn't trust any dame across the street — an' that one least of all. What's she done that makes you trust her?'

'Never mind. Anyway, I've left nothing to chance. The window in that room is boarded up. 'cos there's no glass in it. She can't get out without coming through here. If she tried. we'd hear her trying to move the six-inch nails holding the planks over the window. Right now, she's asleep — or oughta be.'

Ace reflected over this, then he went across to the door and, opening it, walked into the room beyond. Gloria was curled up on a mattress, a blanket thrown over her. There was no bedstead. The mattress lay in a corner not far from the window, through the boards of which daylight filtered, showing up the warps and fissures in the timber.

Ace crept out again and closed the door. He walked over to Steve and cuffed him on the back of his bullet head.

'Get the coffee warmed up Steve and fry some of that canned bacon. And toast. Make it good.'

Steve got up. 'For that dame, d'you mean? I ain't doing it. I fixed breakfast for us, an' if she can't get up in time to have some, I — '

'Fix it!' Ace roared at him.

Steve hesitated, cast a look at the closed door of the girl's room, then turned and went into the hall en route for the back regions. Al put down a queen of Spades and sucked his teeth.

'Better take care how much you play Steve for a mug. boss,' he murmured.

'I can take care of him — and you, too, for that matter — so shut up.'

'Me? I'm not beefin', boss. No need to. But Steve's different. He's got his own ideas, and they might be dangerous.'

'I should worry,' Ace retorted, and resumed his restless pacing up and down the room. He tried the short wave on the radio and got all the news — except that which he wanted. Not a hint of police activity; not a hint of anything.

'Just like we might be dead,' Al said, as Ace shut off the radio again.

'And I don't like it.' Ace lit a cigarette irritably. 'I don't like being left alone. Ain't natural. Makes me feel that the cops may be closing in and saying nothing. I wouldn't put it past McArdel, if he's got the job of tailing us.'

Al considered the table gloomily. 'How long do you reckon we hafta stop here?'

'Depends. Can't send for that guy from Harrisburg until I know where I am, an' it's safe to go out an' use a telephone.'

Steve came back with a tray on which stood a coffeepot, cup and saucer, grilled canned bacon and toast. He dumped it on the table and glared.

'If you expect anything more, boss, don't ask me to do it. I won't — on principle. Y'know what I think about dames being mixed up in our business.'

'What you think don't matter,' Ace told him, and picking up the tray, he balanced it on one hand and took it into the girl's room. She was stirring into wakefulness as he entered. Memories of the previous night were strong upon her. She lay watching, pushing the blonde hair from her face as Ace set the tray on the floor beside her. She made a half move towards his hip pocket, from which the Luger jutted invitingly — but he moved quickly, so she could not follow up her advantage as she wished.

'All for you, honey,' he said, grinning,

as he poured out the coffee. 'Now you an' me are on good terms, you're going to get the best treatment. If either of those mugs out there try anything, just let me know.'

'Uh-huh,' she promised, taking the cup. 'I will.'

He embraced her shoulders with a powerful arm, hugging her to him. She closed her eyes, but was smiling again the moment he released her.

'That's my baby,' he said, rubbing his hands. 'I told you we'd get on swell if we co-operated. You got brains, kid. Just my class.'

Gloria nibbled the toast for a moment, then she asked a question:

'When does something happen? How long do we have to stay around here?'

'Until the heat's off — and it isn't yet. Maybe some days before I can move, and that's what makes me so jittery. Sooner I can get that guy here from Harrisburg and get his wad in exchange for the ice we've got, the better.'

'What makes you so sure you'll be here when that guy comes?' a voice asked coldly from the doorway.

Ace swung round, and the girl looked over his shoulder. Steve was propping the doorpost a gun in his hand a cigarette dangling from his mouth.

'Why, you dirty — ' Ace's hand whipped to his back pocket, but Steve's voice stopped him in mid-action.

'Shouldn't, fella, if I were you. I might have to kill you. Not that I'd mind, but I've a clean record as far as rubbing out is concerned, and I don't want to spit on it now. Get on your feet, the both of you,' he commanded abruptly.

Slowly, Ace obeyed, his face drawn with venom. The girl got up, too, and stood waiting, her hands smoothing down her creased, too-short skirt. Her eyes wandered to Ace's hip pocket, but it was too far away to reach. Steve's eyes pinned her, then moved back to Ace.

'I figger you take me for a sucker, Ace,' he said. 'You must offerin' twenty-five per cent to me and Al, while you take fifty. I'd be crazy to take it. Be more sensible to take the rocks myself and sell 'em to a fence I know in Pittsburg.'

'Get wise to yourself, fella,' Ace told

him. 'For one thing, you don't know where I've hidden those rocks for the time being; and for another, you'd never reach Pittsburg without the cops gettin' you.'

'It's you they're lookin' for, Ace. I'd get by if I hopped a freight train, specially if I had no cases with me. I'd take the stuff sewn up in my coat.'

'You low-down chiseller.' Ace breathed. 'What's the idea of the double-cross? I thought we was all in this together?'

'I don't like being ordered around,' Steve explained sourly. 'Do this. Do that. An' most of it's 'cos of this yellow-haired dame you're draggin' around. I'm not standing for it, Ace. It's too dangerous. I was only waiting till your back was turned, now I'm working' things out me own way. You'll get no help from Al. He's out cold, and trussed.'

Ace looked beyond Steve into the living room. Steve moved a little to one side and gave a view of Al, his head slumped on to his breast, bound to his chair at the table.

'This ain't' goin' to get you anywhere,'

Ace snapped. 'An' I certainly shan't tell you where I've put those cases with the stuff in 'em.'

'Mebbe you will, sooner than you think. I've got it doped out.' Steve moved his gun. 'Get in that room, the both of you — but fast.'

Gloria obeyed, going ahead of Ace. He followed her, tightening his lips as he felt his gun snatched out of his hip pocket. With his hands raised, he stopped at the table watching Steve narrowly. Steve grinned.

'This is one place where the dame comes in useful,' he said. 'I know I'd never find where the stuff is if I had to try and get it outa you; you're too tough. In fact, I wouldn't have tried a double-cross at all if the dame hadn't been here. As it is, I can make it. You think a lot of her, Ace, don't you?'

'Stop monkeyin' around, an' say what you've got to say,' Ace snapped.

'Okay. It's simple enough. Tell me where the stuff is, or the dame takes a beating — like this.' And Steve lashed out his left hand and struck the girl a punishing blow across the face. Unprepared for it, she staggered backwards and collapsed beside the rambling old fireplace.

'You dirty big ape,' Ace said, clenching his fists.

'Shut up an' start talking — an' keep your mitts up.' Steve glanced at the girl as she struggled up. 'Come back here, you.'

Since Steve had a gun in each hand — one pointing at her and the other at Ace — Gloria had no choice. She got on her feet and came over to him.

'Looks like your boyfriend doesn't aim to talk,' he said dryly. 'Mebbe he will before I'm through with you.'

Still keeping her covered, he moved behind Ace amid went over to one of the sashcords hanging from the ancient window. Two one-handed slashes with his knife severed the cord through. He came back to Ace, then, in one swift movement, noosed the cord and drew it taut round Ace's wrists. Gloria saw her chance and dived round the table but, before she could reach his side, Steve's gun was back in his right hand. With his left he picked up Ace's, where — for the moment — he had dropped it to the floor.

'Sit down,' Steve snapped, and gave a shove. His wrists tightly fastened, Ace had to obey. He collapsed in the chair by the table.

'I'll get you for this, Steve,' he breathed venomously. 'You see if I don't.'

Steve took no notice. Reaching out, he snatched the cheap belt from about Gloria's waist. Going behind Ace, he threw the belt about his throat and then drew it taut through the buckle. Ace found his head dragged back, so he was compelled to look towards the ceiling. To try and straighten out played hell with his Adam's apple.

'Now, mebbe we can talk business,' Steve said, as he moved over to the girl. 'Climb on this table, sweetheart, so your boyfriend can see you.'

She did so slowly and stood up, plain fear in her gray eyes. Ace, pinned back in his chair, could see her quite clearly now — every lush line of her. Then Steve came up beside her, his gun bedded in the small of her back.

'What's all this blasted by-play about?' Ace croaked as he strained futilely on the belt and cords. 'I'm not telling you anything about those rocks, either now or any other time.'

'I've decided you will — if you want this dame in one piece. Get this, Ace. I've nothing to lose.' Steve's voice took on the brutal hardness that showed he meant business. 'I've looked this place over everywhere I can, and I can't find them rocks. I've looked the convertible over, too, and they're not there. Start talking before I go to work on this dame.'

Gloria looked at Ace desperately, then at Steve. Not for Ace's sake, but for her own, she had to think of something quickly — but neither idea nor opportunity presented itself.

'See these hooks?' Steve pointed his gun embedded in the main beam. 'This one over the table'll be useful. I'm stringing this moll of yours up to one of 'em unless you talk, Ace. You've one last chance.'

Ace said nothing. The strain of the belt throat felt as though it were breaking his neck. Steve set his ugly mouth.

'Okay, fella — you asked for it. Mebbe your girl will make you talk even yet.'

He jumped down from the table and walked backwards, still keeping his gun trained on Gloria as he went back. From the cupboard of the rickety sideboard he took the towrope that belonged to the convertible; evidently, he had smuggled it in for just this purpose. Slowly, he came back to the table, Gloria watching him narrowly.

And he forgot one thing. She was at a higher level than he, by reason of standing on the table. When he had come within two feet of her she suddenly slammed out her right foot with all her power, straight into his face. He howled with sudden pain as the pointed toe of her shoe cracked right across the bridge of his nose. Nor did she stop there.

Flinging up her hands, she seized the hook immediately overhead and swung her body forward and downward with all the power she had. She crashed into the dazed man and bowled him to the floor. He was aware of her soft but strong young body crushing against him; then she was standing up, aiming the automatic he had dropped, and tossing the hair out of her face.

'Get up, you dirty heel,' she ordered. 'Go on — get up!'

Blood trickling from his cracked nose, Steve obeyed and kept his hands up.

'Nice work, kid,' Ace panted, straining his head to watch her. 'I knew I'd found a dame worth knowing. Get me outa this. I'm damn near choking.'

Gloria hesitated and thought swiftly. She had the gun, and that was something. Before she left this place, she had to know where the stolen stuff was, and take it with her if possible. As an honest member of the community, she considered it her bounden duty.

She moved even as she thought and, still covering Steve with the gun, she unfastened the buckle of the belt that held Ace's neck. He straightened up. Stooping she tugged open the knot which bound his wrists. He stood up slowly and snatched the gun from her.

'Thanks, kid.' He moved a few paces

forward to where Steve was standing, his face blood-streaked from his damaged nose. There was the glint of murder in his eyes.

'Shall I untie Al?' Gloria asked quickly, and she caught the nod Ace gave — then she swung with a gasp and looked over her shoulder as Ace threw down the gun and pushed out his right fist, all in one movement.

Steve took the blow under the chin, jaws snapping together so suddenly he nearly guillotined the end of his tongue. He reeled back against the wall and used it to spring himself forward, his fists clenched. A terrific blow in the stomach doubled him up. Choking hoarsely he stumbled around near the fireplace, then he had to straighten as an uppercut whipped up his head like a punch bag. Half conscious, he toppled backwards and collapsed in a corner, hardly able to breathe.

'Mebbe that'll soften you up a bit, sucker,' Ace told him. 'And you get no cut, either, see?'

He turned and picked up his gun from

101

the table, just as Gloria was looking at it pensively. She gave a little start and met his eyes. It felt like a lead weight descending when she realized she had to play her part for a little while longer yet.

5

'You all right, Al?' Ace asked after a moment, and Al gave a nod as he rubbed the back of his head tenderly for a while.

'Yeah, I'm okay, boss — but I don't know what suddenly got inter Steve.'

'I do. He got ambitious. But he ain't gonna try it any more. He slugged you, didn't he?'

'Sure did. I'd just time to see him coming, and that's all I can remember.'

'All right, then — that means you keep your eye on him henceforth when I'm not doing it. Here's your hardware.'

Ace picked up a fallen automatic from under the table and went over to the half-conscious Steve, tugged his automatic out of his belt and put it on the table beside Al.

'Just in case you need two in a hurry,' Ace explained softly. 'I've got my own. And see you don't get any fancy ideas.'

'You know me, boss.'

'Yeah — that's what has me worried.'

Al looked about him. 'Y'sound as though you're going places, boss, leaving me to watch Steve. What gives?'

'Never mind. I want to talk to Gloria. This way, kid.'

She cast a hopeless look towards the spare gun on the table; wondered if she'd been a fool to throw away her chances, and then followed Ace into the adjoining room, where she had spent the night. He settled on the mattress put his automatic in his hip pocket, then he motioned Gloria to sit beside him.

She obeyed hesitantly, until the pull he gave on her arm forced her down with a bump. She coiled her shapely legs beneath her and tugged at the annoying skirt riding on her knees.

'Listen, kid, what you did back there told me a lot,' Ace said, his black eyes fixed on her. 'You had a chance to walk out on me — even drill me if you wanted — but you didn't. You saved me instead.'

She forced a smile. 'Why shouldn't I?'

Her next move cost her a good deal, but she went ahead just the same. She relaxed her blonde head on Ace's broad shoulder and said nothing as one of his powerful hands snaked gently about her waist.

'You got class, kid,' he murmured. 'More 'n I ever had. I want you to know I appreciate it. Whatever I've got is yours — or will be when we get out of this blasted hole.'

'I've proved I'm on your side, Ace,' she whispered. 'Don't you think it's about time you proved the same about yourself?'

His hand lowered so it rested gently on the smooth curve of her right hip.

'F'r instance?' he asked.

'Those rocks you've hidden. Why not tell me where they are? Then, if things get tough, I might be able to help by knowing just where I can put my hands on them.'

'Sorry, baby; I'm keeping that to myself.'

'You mean you don't trust me?'

Ace gave her a sharp look. Gloria was looking at him under her lashes, her full red mouth petulant. He gave a sudden grin and kissed her. She took it and didn't move a muscle.

'It isn't I don't trust you,' he said. 'It's just that that stuff is hot — too hot for a gal like you to handle if there should be trouble. You're safer not knowing.'

She sighed. Ace drew her more tightly to him, his hand straying from her hip so that it dropped idly between her knees. She moved, and he looked surprised.

'Anything wrong, kid? You didn't budge last night.'

'That was last night,' she said, and made an effort to get up. Ace's hands shifted and locked beneath her waist, pinning her to him. She forced his hands away and got on her feet. Going over to the window, she peered through the chinks.

'Sorry, kid, about the rocks,' he said. 'That's my business, much as I like you.'

Gloria did not say anything. She still maintained her aggrieved expression. Ace sat looking at her. No matter what position she stood in, she looked the real thing.

She was trying to work out in her own mind just how it might be possible to make him talk. Once she knew where the stuff was, a little playing up to him might easily bring the automatic into her hand, even if it cost her plenty in personal respect.

'It was a brainwave, taking that dress, kid.' Ace said with a grin and she gave a start, realizing that her stance was such that it threw every line of her limbs into relief in the filtered sunlight.

She moved restlessly, hugging herself gently. She paused after a brief walk round and stopped a foot or so from Ace. He looked up at her with a half quizzical expression.

'Suppose Steve gets fighting mad again?' she questioned. 'Just suppose he does? If by some chance he wiped you out — and Al, too — there'd only be me left. Deep down he thinks I know where that stuff is. If I did know I could save myself being killed by inches. If I don't, he might do — just anything to me.'

'Y'don't have to worry about Steve, kid. He's taken care of. Al will watch him.'

'How do you know you can trust Al?'

'Because he knows what's good for

him. He ain't like Steve. Steve's a dirty sadist — an' stop worryin', will you? Come an be friendly, and stop walkin' around.'

'I'd sooner have something to eat,' Gloria said. 'I didn't get any breakfast, remember? Steve interrupted us.'

Ace gave a start. 'Yeah — so he did. I'll fix that right now. I'm kinda hungry myself, come to think of it. Stay here and I'll go fix something.'

Ace scrambled to his feet and left the room. Gloria watched the door close and gave a little shudder to herself. She felt like someone defiled.

* * *

After the meal and, indeed, through the hot, wearying day and part of the evening, she tried by indirect methods to get Ace to speak, without success. So, for the time being, she had to give up before he became too suspicious.

In this time, Steve had recovered himself. The traces of his hammering wasted away under the cold water tap, he sat in a corner of the main room, passing no remarks; but the cold, homicidal stare in his eyes were speaking his thoughts plainly. Al kept him under constant surveillance, his automatic ready for action.

Now and again Ace tried the radio amid got nothing, insofar as it was of interest, at least. Gloria coiled herself up on the divan and smoked endless cigarettes. It was the kind of atmosphere in which anything might happen — and, at nightfall, as Ace was lighting the oil-lamp, something did.

Gloria herself noticed it first. She had gone to the window facing the driveway, intending to draw the drapes. She stared out into the deep twilight and started back. A powerful black car had jerked to a standstill outside the big gates. Perhaps the police — and if so it would be better if she kept quiet.

'What in heck are you delayin' about, kid?' Ace demanded, striding over to her. 'We don't want this light to be — '

He broke off, staring intently into the gloom outside.

'Hell!' he said, and the way he said it brought Al and Steve to attention. 'Why the heck didn't you tell me that car had just driven up — ?'

'I — I didn't know what to think,' Gloria hesitated.

'Cops?' Al asked sharply.

Ace pulled the drapes over quickly. 'Nope. From the looks of it, it's 'Fingers' and his boys. I'd know that sedan of his anywhere. Guess he must have seen this light, too. He knows we're here.'

''Fingers'?' Al repeated blankly. 'How in heck did he know we're here?'

'I dunno — but we're blowin' quick. Not enough of us to take care of that bunch.'

Ace swung and darted out of the room, across the hall. Gloria stood looking about her blankly, wondering what to do next. Then she ducked as the glass in the window shattered before a bullet. Al got up too, covering Steve. There was the sound of hurrying feet, and Ace came flying in from the hall. He had the two hide cases of valuables in one hand and his automatic in the other. Obviously, he had dug the stuff from its hiding place.

'Out!' he snapped. 'Follow me — out the back way before things get too hot. No time for the car. Have to hoof it.'

He swung back into the hall and Al dived after him Gloria made to go too but instead, she met up a fist that struck her violently on the jaw. She slewed round and dropped to the hard floor, face down. When she had shaken the daze out of her brain, she looked around, to find Steve closing the bolts over the door that led into the hall. He grinned malevolently at her in the light of the oil lamp.

'One trick Ace didn't make, sister,' he explained. 'He can't come back for you — not with 'Fingers' and his crowd outside, and him carrying all that ice. He'll hafta keep going, same as Al will. That leaves you an' me — an' after I've fought it out with 'Fingers', I'll pay you back for that kick in the nose you gave me.'

He swung and dived for the window, keeping to one side of it. Nosing the drapes back slightly with the automatic Al had left on the table, he fired twice.

Somebody fired back and more glass went. Gloria struggled up from the floor and looked around her desperately. Then she dived for the door.

Steve was upon her immediately. Whirling her round he forced her backwards until she reached the table. Pinning her down by main strength, he whipped up the tow rope from the floor, which he'd intended to use earlier, and began to bind her ankles and then her wrists swiftly. Finally, he tied them together, so she lay face down and helplessly struggling on the table top.

Steve looked across at the oil lamp on the sideboard, then fired savagely at the window as a gun blazed at him from there. From outside came a brief scream, and the shooting stopped.

Just how many men were outside Steve did not know — but he did know he couldn't hold all of them. He swung back to Gloria.

'I'm leavin' you a goodbye present, sweetheart,' he said bitterly. 'I hope it works out the way I figger it to. I'm gettin' outa here and leavin' you to enjoy yourself. If you're wonderin' why, it's because it's the only way I can make Ace smart. He's fond of you; to lose you will make him sore. That's my way of gettin' my own back, see? He said he'd give me no cut — so there was no point in following him — and you didn't, neither. I saw to that.'

He swung round abruptly, took the oil lamp from the sideboard and dashed it on the floor under the table. It burst into flame immediately, and Gloria struggled with doubled intensity as black smoke gushed upwards, surging into her lungs.

Steve swung round to the shattered window and had a swift peep outside. He could not see anybody. He cast one look back at the flames seizing a hold of the wooden floor amidst the burning oil, then he gripped the automatic firmly and climbed through the window with caution.

He began crossing the weed-choked flowerbed — then he came face to face in the gloom with a looming figure. He tried to fire, but he wasn't quick enough. A bullet tore like white-hot lead into his stomach. He choked and gasped over the deadly pain; then he had no more need to worry as another slug got him right through the heart. Mugsy chuckled in the gloom and cast a glance at the flickering red visible inside the room where the drapes had been pushed aside by Steve's recent departure.

Speeding feet in the gloom checked his movement. 'Fingers', in evening dress and a black overcoat, homburg on one side of his head, came hurrying up.

'What goes on?' he demanded. 'Haven't you boys cleaned this job up yet? How many more left inside?'

'Dunno, boss,' Mugsy answered. 'Joe, back there, got himself turned into a stiff. I don't know where Harry is. I caught this guy sneakin' out. I guess Ace, the girl and the other guy must still be inside, an' others there might be, too.'

'Time we looked.' 'Fingers' snapped. 'The place is on fire from the look of things. Find the rest of our boys: I'll look inside here.'

He tugged out his automatic and

advanced to the window drapes, tugging them to one side. He gave a start of surprise at the sight of Gloria struggling frantically on the table top. One of its legs was burning already.

He hesitated no longer. Clambering quickly through the window, he hurried across to the girl and picked her up bodily in his arms, bound as she was. Coughing and spluttering, he carried her through the smoke-clogged room to the freshness of the air beyond the window.

'Thanks,' she panted hoarsely, as he slashed through the cords with his knife when he'd put her on her feet. 'I thought I was finished that time.'

'Quiet,' 'Fingers' interrupted suddenly. 'Quiet a minute.'

Gloria waited, surprised; then she understood what had caught his attention. On the still night air there had come the ever-deepening throbbing of a powerful car.

'Cops,' he said abruptly, seizing her arm. 'Coming over the rise. Can't be anybody else in this part — let's go.'

He hurried her through the gloom,

tripping and falling, and within seconds they had gained his sedan. She fell in at one side whilst he dropped at the steering wheel.

'What — what about your men?' she asked in surprise, as he switched on the ignition.

'They must look out for themselves. I've got to get outa here at all costs — ' and he shot the car forward, its lights extinguished, into the gloom. Not fifteen seconds later, Captain McArdel tumbled out of the police car at the gates of the burning house, the sergeant and three police officers with him.

'Go to it, boys,' he ordered. 'Dig out all you can — and where in hell have they parked that sedan they were using?'

He looked about him in vain. At that moment, 'Fingers'' sedan was a mile away from McArdel — but its black, breakneck progress along the country road was seen by Ace and Al as they hurried across a field.

'That 'Fingers'' car?' Al asked, after it had gone by.

Ace led the way on to the roadway

116

before he replied. In each hand he carried one of the hide cases.

'Sure was. I'd know it anywhere. How many of his boys were in it? Did you see?'

'Guess not. Too dark. All of 'em, I suppose.'

Ace hesitated. 'Now he's gone, I'm goin' back, Al. Steve musta got Gloria at the last moment; nice timin'. He knew I couldn't get back while 'Fingers' and his boys were around. I've gotta get her.'

'Yeah?' Al's voice was grim. 'Take a look at that, now.'

Ace looked. Across the fields they had covered lay a pulsating red glow. Though the house that had been their hideout was concealed from here by a rise in the land, they both knew what the glare meant.

'Some of 'Fingers'' work, I reckon,' Ace breathed. 'By hell, I'll get him for this later. That was the best hideout I ever had.'

'S'posin' the dame's in there?' Al demanded. 'Or Steve?'

Ace was silent for a moment. He was accustomed to adjusting himself quickly to the unexpected.

'I reckon we just can't do anything about it now — even if we went back. If Steve's in that, he deserves it all; but it's tough about the gal. She was a nice kid.' He deliberately turned his back on the glow. 'We've gotta keep goin'.'

'Where to? Now we've been slung outa that joint, I don't give a red nickel for our chances.'

'We'll get by. We've got to. Worth tryin', ain't it? One less now to share this stuff with when I can contact that guy from Harrisburg.'

'Yeah. When!'

They started moving along the solitary high road. They had been going for perhaps ten minutes when the sound of a powerful car engine gave them pause. They both swung round in alarm, startled to find the approaching car was nearer than they had thought. They both dived for the long grass at the side of the road and, at the same instant, blinding headlights burst upon them.

With a screech, the car swept to a halt. There was the roar of a man's voice. The crack of a gun followed it. Ace went blundering on wildly in the gloom, his precious cases still in his hands. One brief glance back showed him dim figures chasing after him. Al was at his side, breathing hard. A gun exploded again. Al groaned, stumbled and dropped.

'Hey, you!' bellowed a voice, and Ace heard a slug whang past his ear.

He kept on blindly running, gasping for breath, tripping over grass tufts, getting up again — keeping low down so the skyline would not show him. He twisted and detoured and crouched, only slowing down at last when he gained the outskirts of a small but dense wood that enveloped him completely.

Breathing desperately, his lungs stinging, he drew himself into deep shadow and waited. Perspiration was pouring down his face; his hair was matted. The cases felt as though their handles had stuck to his palms.

'Skunks,' he whispered. 'Dirty, low-down skunks! Chase a guy as though he was an animal.'

Little by little, he began to cool down. The pursuing police had evidently completely lost track of him. From this position, he could not see the road, but eventually — nearly an hour afterwards, he reckoned — he heard the bass throbbing of the police car start up again and then gradually fade into the distance. He grinned to himself crookedly.

'Which leaves me alone,' he muttered. 'Al took it on the lam; Steve's out. Even the gal's out — pity.' He shook his head. 'She was one swell kid.'

He stood thinking in the darkness. He had got to get food and drink somewhere while he planned out what to do next. He thought back on something Steve had said — about carrying the rocks in his clothes and dumping the cases. He got to work on the idea; transferred the rings and various items of jewelry to his pockets and the inside of his shirt — then he threw the cases away and, automatic in hand, went on through the wood. When it ended, he found himself looking at the dark countryside — but not very far away were two yellow rectangles of light. Evidently some remote farmstead. He began moving resolutely towards it.

A dog barked somewhere as he reached the yard. He ignored it and walked over to the porchway, knocking heavily on the screen door. After a moment a lighted lamp appeared, a girl of perhaps fourteen carrying it. She opened the screen door and looked into the night.

'Take it easy, kid,' Ace whispered, prodding the gun dead in the center of the youngster's midriff. 'How many folks here besides you?'

'Only — only m-my mother and d-dad,' the girl faltered, her eyes wide.

'Yeah? Good!' The girl had chestnut hair and a wholesome country look about her, Ace decided. He took the lamp from her — then her father's voice came from the living room.

'Who is it, Mary?'

'I'll take care of this.' Ace said 'Go right ahead of me.'

The girl obeyed, the gun in her back. Ace found himself in a big, comfortable living room where twin oil lamps burned on the table and a middle-aged man and woman sat before a fire, the man reading, the woman darning.

'Nice, homely set-up,' Ace commented dryly, and nudged the girl to one side, leveling his gun. 'Sorry to bust in.'

The man jumped up, powerful, fury in his tanned face.

'What in tarnation does this mean? Who are you?'

'Never mind. Don't bother askin' questions, pop, because I don't aim to answer them. Rustle me some food together, an' make it quick. An' coffee.'

The woman, too, was on her feet now, astounded. The girl drifted over to her parents and stood looking in awe at Ace's gun.

'A stick-up, huh?' the farmer demanded. 'Won't do you any good. There's nothing here worth you attention, friend.'

Ace eyed him. 'Don't get me wrong, pop. I'm not here to frisk, but to get some food. I'm on the run, see? You'll know all about it soon enough, so there's no harm in me tellin' you. But I'm warnin' you — try anything, or give any hint that I'm here, an' you'll be short of a daughter. I figger that's what she said she is.'

'You — you'd shoot Mary, do you

mean?' the woman asked, in horror.

'If I had to teach you a lesson, yeah — sure I would. Otherwise, she's in the clear, an' so are you. Now get me somethin' to eat an' make it quick.'

The farmer jerked his head to the girl. She nodded and went into the back regions. Ace could see her shadow on the wall as she lighted another oil lamp. He put down the one he was holding on the nearby dresser, crossed to the table, then sank down wearily in the chair in front of it. Without a word, the woman came across, took a cloth from the dresser, then spread it over the table. Ace sat watching morosely as she set out a plate, knife and fork, and all the necessities of a meal.

'You slick guys who get on the run don't show much sense, do you?' the farmer asked dryly. 'Put yourself through hell, just for some money you're not entitled to. Mug's game, fella.'

Ace aimed him a grim look. 'S'pose you let me worry about that? — and hurry the meal up.'

'It'll be here,' the woman said placidly.

'Mary's warming up some stew.'

Ace said no more and, presently, the girl brought the stew in and set it before him. The coffee pot followed it. Ace began his meal, his automatic on the table beside him. Silently the farmer and his wife and daughter retired to the fireplace and sat watching him.

'D'you hafta stare at me like that?' he demanded. 'I'm not a blasted curio, am I?'

'Nope,' the farmer said, lighting his pipe. 'Just a sucker, that's all. They'll get you in the end, fella, and you know it. I guess you're running from something big at that. Would it be murder?'

'No, it wouldn't. I never murdered anybody in my life. That's one thing I stop at. The rap's too tough.'

The farmer said nothing. He had an unnerving habit of staring intently, as though trying to size something up. His wife picked up her darning and continued to bodge the needle as though nothing had happened. Ace went on eating. His eyes shifted to the girl. She was sitting on a low stool beside the fire, her white-socked feet curled round the back of the stool legs. She was younger than Ace had thought — perhaps no more than twelve. A kitten played in her lap. About her hips, she was nicely rounded.

'Looks like you don't take me seriously,' Ace said at length, his voice sour.

'Meaning?' The farmer drew at his pipe steadily.

'You ain't bothered about me bein' here. This ain't bubble-gum on the table here, remember? It's a Luger automatic. It can kill.'

The farmer smiled a little 'Danger ain't nothing new to us, fella; we're always fighting it — not in the form you've brought it; but from the weather, pests, and illness. We take things as they come.'

'I can see that.' Ace chewed deliberately, then took a draught from his coffee cup. He couldn't weigh up the angle. First time he hadn't struck terror. Probably the old guy was waiting to pull something. It came to Ace as a shock when he realized he wouldn't dare sleep.

One second off guard and anything could happen.

'How long do you think of staying?' the woman said presently, without looking up.

'Till I'm good an' ready to go.'

'Up to you. Men will be here tomorrow — busy on the farm. They might ask questions. They're the sort of men who won't be stopped by that gun of yours. I'd advise you, fella, to just keep on running. You're welcome to the meal. Reckon it's only Christian, even if you are on the run. None of us is perfect, I reckon.'

Ace stared at her in wonder. Nobody had ever said anything that nice to him in his life before. The youngster on the stool put the kitten down and, with the carelessness of youth, sat with her mind a blank, thinking. Ace contemplated her. Only a kid yet, sure. There'd come a time when a guy would come along and like her. She'd have limbs good as Gloria's one day. One day — one —

With a savage effort, Ace caught himself out in a half doze. He jumped a little. The girl was at his side, her eyes wide and the light catching her magnificent chestnut hair.

'Do you want some more coffee, mister?' she asked

Ace nodded. Mustn't go to sleep. Mustn't go — to — sleep . . .

6

It was after midnight when 'Fingers' drove into the town. He had made so many detours from Loyalsock that Gloria was completely bewildered. He had spoken little, too, on the journey, so she had no idea what was ahead of her. She knew from Ace that his name was 'Fingers', but had gotten no further. Things only started to make sense when he pulled the big sedan in a side alley and jammed on the brakes. Gloria looked out on to a solitary wall sign that said: 'SILVER SLIPPER' — EMERGENCY DOOR.

'Your place?' she asked, as he opened the car door.

'Uh-huh. Out you get. We've things to discuss.'

In the alleyway he came hurrying round the car and took her arm. He led her into a dimly-lighted passageway, up a flight of back stairs, and so into his office.

Somewhere on the journey she had heard the strains of a jive orchestra.

'Take a seat.' 'Fingers' invited, switching on the light; and he hung up his overcoat and hat and came over to his desk. He cast a look at her on his way.

Despite the ridiculous dress, despite the dirt on her face and half-bare arms, she had looks and quality. And those smoke-gray eyes, with the long lashes, had something, too.

'You're 'Fingers', I suppose?' she asked, taking a cigarette from the box he held out.

' 'Fingers' Baxter to be exact. I got the nickname 'cos I like my mitts well manicured.' He held out his immaculate hands. 'I s'pose you're the dame Ace has been running around with?'

'I'm Gloria Vane, small-time movie actress.'

'You oughta be big-time, baby, with that face and upholstery. Tell me what happened. I think I can help you.'

Gloria told him. She felt she couldn't be any worse off than she had been with Ace — and anyway, she was in New York now and more or less free to move about. 'Fingers' wasn't half bad, either. He looked polished. His blond hair was attractive; so were his blue eyes. Pity his mouth was like a steel trap.

'So that's the set-up?' he mused. 'An' you've no idea where Ace hid that stuff he frisked?'

'None. In any case, it doesn't signify now. When he saw you coming, he moved fast and took the stuff with him.'

'Fingers' made a grimace. 'Which means I've got to go right on looking for him. Anyway, that's my business. I went out to Loyalsock for no other reason than to get that stuff. Instead, I got you. Not so sure I mind, either.'

Gloria met his eyes steadily. 'I've had trouble with one tinhorn, 'Fingers'. I don't feel like starting with another.'

He grinned round his cigarette. 'You don't have to class me with that gorilla, Ace Monohan,' he said. 'He never was anythin' but a cheap crook; but even a cheap one can cramp your style some-times, which is why I want to put the finger on him. No, Gloria, I'm a businessman. Interested in dollars, not dames — though I'm not sucker enough to say that I don't like a pretty face.'

'Which adds up to what?'

'As I said at first, I think I can help you. When you were heading for New York here and ran into Ace, what were your plans?'

'Hazy. I was going to see my agent and see if I could fix myself up with a new movie assignment.'

'I could use you as the high spot in my floor show, if you can sing or dance.'

'I can do both. I'm also an acrobatic contortionist. I'm not terrific, but I get by,' Gloria said, and then added: 'Any strings?'

'None,' 'Fingers' answered. 'Like I told you — women as such don't interest me. My particular concern with you is that you know a lot about me; therefore, it will pay me to keep you comfortable. I don't suppose the fact of my saving your life will make you swear undying allegiance, so I'll add something more concrete. You get the floor show job, a good salary, and I can fix you up in an apartment house I own, rent-free. Okay?'

'Sounds it,' Gloria admitted. 'But I still can't see you doing all that without sending the bill in later.'

'You've been running around with Ace too long,' 'Fingers' told her dryly. 'All I want you to do is play the game my way — even when the police come nosin' around — as they will. When they know I started that attack on Ace, they'll be here to ask plenty of questions, chiefly because I couldn't have known where Ace was without it tying up with a girl who was murdered.'

Gloria looked puzzled, and 'Fingers' motioned a hand.

'Don't try and figger it out, Gloria; it's too complicated. Just remember one thing when the police question you: I saved you from being burned to death. That's all.'

'And — and that's the sum total of everything you want from me?'

'For the present.' 'Fingers' got to his feet. 'I'm glad you're willing to play ball, Gloria, it won't do you any harm, believe me: Right now you look all in. Think you can hang on long enough for me to show you your apartment? Then you can do as you like till eleven tomorrow morning. I'll want you then to meet my floor show manager.'

'After the treatment I got from Ace, you seem like something out of a story book,' Gloria said, rising and, taking down his hat and coat from the stand, he opened the door for her.

★   ★   ★

At Sixth Precinct Headquarters, Homicide Division, Mugsy was taking it on the lamp. He sat sweating before the glare of twin floodlights, peering uselessly into the surrounding dark and listening to machine-gun questions.

'Listen, Mugsy — why make things tough for yourself? You've already admitted 'Fingers' led that raid on the house in Loyalsock because he knew Ace was hiding there — so why not tell us how 'Fingers' got his information? Come on — quick.'

'I'm sayin' no more,' Mugsy panted. 'Let me alone, can't you?'

'You got the information from a girl called Betty Hopson. Didn't you?'

'No. No, I didn't. I never heard of the dame.'

'Yes, you did, Mugsy. You strung her up in a warehouse after she'd talked.'

Mugsy's eyes darted about him desperately. He couldn't see anybody. There was only the glare and the implacable voices.

'Better tell us Mugsy, or you're going to be here an awful long time.'

Mugsy breathed hard and sweated some more. He choked over his next words.

'It was 'Fingers', I tell you. He told me to do it. I had to do it!'

'Never mind 'Fingers'. You murdered Betty Hopson. Didn't you? *Didn't you*? Trussed her up so she couldn't move. Stuck a gag in her mouth. Put a rope round her neck and hanged her. *You* did that, didn't you? Of your own free will?'

' 'Fingers' told me to!' Mugsy shrieked, banging his chair arms. 'I had to rub her out — '

' 'Fingers' didn't give you the rope, did he? He didn't say how you were to rub

134

her out, did he?'

'No — no!' Mugsy gave a groan. 'Okay — okay — I killed her. I didn't want to, but it was my job to blot her out. The river was too far, an' a rope was handy.'

Silence. The crushing brilliance and not a thing that moved. Mugsy stared into the blaze like a blind man.

'What in hell more d'you want? I've admitted it, ain't I? Get me outa here! I can't stand this light — '

'Shut up, Mugsy. You're not through yet. You shot Steve Moran tonight, didn't you — out at Loyalsock?'

'I — I — '

'Right in the belly, Mugsy. Better come clean. We checked the slug with your gun. You shot him.'

'Yeah,' Mugsy whispered, dragging a hand over his sweating face. 'Yeah, I shot the guy. Don't matter. I've admitted one killing; another can't make any difference, I guess.'

'How much do you know about Ace and his boys, and that girl, Gloria Vane?'

'I don't know anything about 'em. You've gotta believe that. I don't!'

'We don't believe it,' stated the voice — hard, merciless. 'You know something about that girl! You set fire to that house, didn't you? Mebbe to burn up the girl — '

'Why'd I want to do that?' Mugsy shouted. 'She didn't mean anything to me! The house started fryin' after we'd gotten there. Somebody inside musta done it. Last I saw of the boss, he was goin' through the window — '

'He was huh? Then he ratted on you afterwards?'

'Yeah, yeah. He took a powder — left me an' the boys. Musta been him. 'cos the rest of our boys were with me. I'd gone to find 'em.'

'How do you know that it wasn't Ace pulling a fast one.'

'It — it could ha' bin,' Mugsy admitted, scowling. 'Mebbe the boss went up in smoke.'

'All right, boys,' Captain McArdel's voice interrupted. 'Take him out.'

The floods expired. The normal office lighting then seemed dirty yellow to Mugsy as he was hauled to his feet. He didn't struggle as he was bundled out of the office by two strong-arm cops. McArdel lounged to his desk and stood thinking, two plainclothes men and the sergeant grouped about him.

'That pins Mugsy for the murder rap as far as Betty Hopson's concerned, anyway,' he said at length. 'On the other hand, it looks as though Ace had gotten away with it for the time being. We got Al, but not him. Since we know it wasn't Ace who took the sedan, it must have been 'Fingers'. I'll gamble when he went in that burning house he found Gloria Vane and took her away quick when he saw us coming. He ditched his boys and got clear — about the only move he could make right then. That means Gloria Vane may be tied up-with him. It's just possible she might know where Ace is hiding out.'

'Possible,' the sergeant agreed, 'but I doubt it. He probably didn't know himself where he was going to settle.'

'I'll have a talk with the girl, anyway,' McArdel said.

'Now?'

'Nope. It'll do in the morning. For one

thing, 'Fingers' would probably take a long way round to get into town, to avoid being seen, and he mightn't have got back even yet; for another, we're only human, and we need sleep as much as anybody else. Wherever Ace is, a few more hours can't hurt. All we can hope for is that the dragnet we've left around Loyalsock will do some good, and nail him. I guess he can't go on for ever.'

★   ★   ★

Ace himself was very much aware of this fact at almost the time McArdel was speaking. He was still at the table, the meal long since finished, a cigarette now dangling from the corner of his mouth. Only the farmer remained awake. His wife had fallen asleep in her chair; the girl had stretched herself on the sofa in the corner and was dead off.

'What kind of a blasted game d'you call this, fella?' the farmer demanded at last. 'Is there any reason why my wife and the kid can't go to bed properly?'

'Every reason!' Ace snapped. 'Once

they're outa my sight, they might do just anything. I ain't takin' that chance. They could escape through the bedroom window to the outside and go an' tell the cops couldn't they? Or they could signal with a lamp — lots of things they could do. Let 'em stay here. It's safer.'

The farmer shrugged, stirred the low fire into a blaze, then sat looking into the flames. Ace's eyes moved up to the busy little clock on the mantle. It said one-fifteen, and he was as sleepy as all hell. Probably the meal he had eaten, and the warmth of the room. He dare not succumb. It might be the end of him.

With an effort, he got to his feet. The farmer looked at him in surprise.

'I'm goin',' Ace said briefly. 'Got to be on my way — an' I'm warnin' you. If you spill it to the cops that I've been here. I'll be back an' get you or the kid there.'

The farmer said nothing and Ace knew quite well he had made an empty threat. The farmer would talk; that was inevitable. As for taking care of him if he did — utterly impossible, of course.

Ace turned, going out backwards, with

his automatic leveled; then, the moment he was out of sight of the farmer, he slipped the gun in his pocket, hurried across the main hall and gained the outdoors. The fresh night air revived him immediately. He began to hurry away from the farm in the starlight, striking out towards the spot where — remotely distant — he could see the faint red plume that denoted a railway track. It was his only chance; to hop a freight, get to a fresh town, and lose himself.

Then, as he went, new ideas began to form. In other cities, the cops would probably be on the lookout for him. They'd keep tabs on freight trains, road transport, and every other means a guy on the run might use. What would happen, though, if he went right back — under their noses? Where he had friends, who'd keep him low until the heat was really off? What was wrong in returning to his own happy hunting ground of New York City?

He grinned at the notion; then another thought struck him. He knew beyond doubt that 'Fingers' had been behind that attack on the house, but he did not know what had happened to 'Fingers' — and if that slick guy had returned to town he had an account to settle. Because of him, Gloria had been lost, probably killed. Yeah — the dirty bum had a lot to answer for.

That settled it for Ace. He'd get back to N.Y.C., wait until he'd gathered all his facts, and then act. In the meantime, he might be able to get word through to that fence in Harrisburg.

But things were not as easy as all that. He caught a New York-bound freighter okay, and landed himself in with half a dozen other hombres getting transport on the cheap — but the farmer had been busy in the meantime, setting out to advise the local police — a journey of some three miles in his jalopy — the moment Ace had turned his back.

Wires had begun to hum immediately. The dragnet operation at Captain McArdel's order tightened a deal. Road and rail transport came in for sudden intense scrutiny. A hold-up murderer was trying to make a getaway, and had got to be found. Because of this, the freighter, headed for New York, was stopped just outside Flemington, on the Pennsylvania-New Jersey border.

Ace, who had been dozing in the dark amidst a pile of bales, was aware of the slowing down and, for a moment, or two, took it to be signals. Then he heard some of the men in the darkness muttering amongst themselves excitedly.

'Ain't usual to stop here, right on the bridge.'

'You said it, bud. Never happened before, I guess.'

Ace got to his feet and felt his way to where the men were talking in the darkness.

'What gives?' he asked sharply.

'You hot, fella?' one of the men asked.

'Plenty.'

'Then you'd better watch yourself. I can think of only one reason for this stoppage right here — an' that's cops. Come to think of it,' the man added, 'it ain't goin' to be so pleasant for any of us, either.'

Ace stumbled over to the sliding doors and moved them aside very gently. He looked out into gray moonlight and the X-like girders of a bridge. Far below flowed the sheen of a river. He listened intently. The distant engine was snorting steam at intervals. There were shouts — from men, coming nearer and as they came they were evidently turning out illegal passengers. Ace could see them tumbling out on the line and waiting. Being on a bridge, there was no escape. Just like the blasted cops to think of that!

'Cops is right,' Ace breathed, glancing back at the man who was straining to look over his shoulder. 'An' I'm not stayin' to pass the time of day, neither.'

He eased his automatic into his hand, then leapt down to the up railroad. The noise he made landing amidst the clinkers was plain enough for the not far distant men to hear. They began hurrying towards him, knowing full well that no ordinary freight-jumper would try to escape like this. They always submitted quietly, and did the same trick again when they'd done their bit for the one before it.

This was different. The guy was

running for it — and running fast. Refreshed from his sleep, Ace stumbled and slipped on the clinkers and wooden sleepers. He heard a powerful voice yell at him:

'Hold it, you mug, or you'll get it in the back!'

Ace didn't hold it. He had too much regard for freedom and he hoped the light was too bad for a dead shot. A revolver exploded. The slug hit the rail beside him and twanged like a hawser under strain. Another bullet followed, blasting dirt a few inches from his feet.

Ace glanced over his shoulder. Firing back would do no good. The guys would be on him before he could take aim; and if he did not stop, they'd get him for sure as they hurtled nearer. He thought as he traveled — then he veered right, jumping the gleaming metals, and reached the steel parapet of the bridge. He leapt — out and out. Down, down, down, until he thought his heart was going to force itself through the top of his head. He landed and plunged under the water, then began to rise again almost immediately.

The cops on the bridge above stood at the rail, staring over. One of them whistled and cuffed up his uniform cap.

'I guess it might ha' been Ace at that. These guys don't run like that without a reason — an' they don't take a dive like this, either. See him down there? That speck in the water?'

'Yeah. No use shootin' from this distance. Better phone back to headquarters. He's gotta come outa the water some time. Makes you think, the risks these mugs take, just because they won't earn an honest living.'

So the information was later phoned back to headquarters and the police in the district concerned, including the river police, kept themselves alert for some sign of the slippery Ace. The following morning, Captain McArdel got the news, too, in New York. There was nothing he could do about it right then, it was up to the men in the area where Ace had last been seen — but there was something else he could do — and he did.

At ten o'clock, he walked into the 'Silver Shipper' and was told 'Fingers' had not arrived. Undeterred, he sat down in the emptiness of the nightspot and just watched the men with their mops and dusters. It was a quarter to eleven when 'Fingers' showed up, immaculate as usual, just drawing off his yellow gloves. If he was at all put off-key by the sight of Captain McArdel waiting for him, he did not betray it.

'You again, huh?' he asked, stopping at the table where McArdel was seated. 'What gives this time? I never seem to get you out of my hair.'

'Yeah — annoying, isn't it?' McArdel asked dryly, getting up. 'Let's go up to your office. I want a word with you.'

'Fingers' shrugged and led the way across the dimly-lighted expanse. The elevator took them upstairs. Once in the office, 'Fingers' put his hat on the stand and then went over to his desk, folding his gloves neatly afterwards.

'This talk goin' to be chatty enough to warrant a smoke?' he asked sourly.

'Smoke all you want. 'Fingers'. Count me out. I'm on duty — very much so.'

'Yeah? Seems to consist of chasin' me

around most of the time — an' I don't have to tell you again that I don't like it, do I?'

'Fingers' settled in his swivel chair and lit his cigarette. McArdel stood eyeing him narrowly.

'Quit the stalling. 'Fingers',' he said at length. 'You don't fool anybody but yourself. I know all about that stunt you pulled last night — the one that blasted Monohan into the open, and cost him his two remaining boys at the same time.'

'I pulled?' 'Fingers' repeated insolently. 'If you can't prove that, you're on dangerous ground, copper.'

'I can prove it. Mugsy told me all about it.'

'Fingers' was silent for several moments; then he shrugged.

'He did, huh? Mugsy's a cheapskate, but he's got his own ideas of loyalty. I'll gamble you had to grill him pretty hard to get that much outa him.'

'He talked,' McArdel said. 'That's all that matters. Right now, he's pinned with a double murder rap — Betty Hopson's and Steve Moran's.'

147

'That bonehead? I reckon Mugsy has done everybody a service, blotting him out.'

'Murder, just the same, 'Fingers'. I don't have to tell you that. From here on, you can take Mugsy off your payroll.'

'Fingers' glanced impatiently at his wristwatch. It was ten to eleven.

'Look, McArdel, I've more things to do than just sit around talking to you. What's all this about? You nailed Mugsy; you know I had a smack at Ace Monohan in Loyalsock. Okay! There's nothing you can do about it. I'm not the hold-up man from the Filanti job. That's Ace. Me chasin' him doesn't mean a thing.'

'It would have done, if you'd have got his stuff from him.'

'I didn't — an' I don't know where he is. So where does this get us?'

McArdel sat down and crossed his legs. 'I'm looking for Gloria Vane, and I think you know where she is.'

'Yeah? You always did get queer ideas, fella.'

'There's an abduction charge, 'Fingers'. It's out for Ace, as well as a murder charge, and if you've taken Gloria from Ace, it's out for you as well.'

'Fingers' laughed shortly. 'You can't make that charge stick, McArdel.'

'I think I can. The law doesn't agree with people taking other people away against their will. You'd better tell me what you know about Gloria — and Ace, too — before I find it out the hard way. You can't spar with the police for ever, remember.'

'I haven't the vaguest idea where the dame is — or Ace, either,' 'Fingers' snapped.

'I'll make a guess, 'Fingers'. Mugsy saw you climb into that house when it was burning. My guess is you found Gloria Vane in there. If she was dead. then I've got to pin a murder and arson charge on somebody, and — '

'Arson?'

'That's what I said. Ace may be a crook, but he bought that house with straight money. We've found that out. That means if anybody burns it down, they can be accused of arson — and will be.'

'The law sure is crazy,' 'Fingers' reflected.

'If, on the other hand you found Gloria Vane alive.' McArdel continued 'and forced her to escape with you, that makes you guilty of abduction — '

McArdel stopped at a tap on the door. Gloria herself came in. 'Fingers' looked at her, then at his watch, and his steel-trap mouth set hard. The girl hesitated, looking from one to the other. They sat looking at her. In a new dress and a saucy hat, she looked the last word.

McArdel got to his feet. 'You Miss Vane?' he asked briefly.

'I — er — ' Gloria hesitated, then nodded. 'Yes, I am.'

'Thanks for the confirmation. I was just checking up on the photographs I have of you from your agent.'

'Oh — '

'I'm Captain McArdel, Homicide,' McArdel added, and shook hands. 'I was just asking 'Fingers' about you.'

'Grilling me would be nearer,' 'Fingers' growled.

'You've nothing more to fear, Miss Vane,' McArdel said. 'You walking in here has saved me a lot of trouble looking for you. If you want your wrecked car, it's at the City Garage. As for you yourself, you're a free citizen again.'

The girl caught a look from 'Fingers'. She faced McArdel again.

'I became a free citizen the moment I escaped Ace Monohan, Captain. 'Fingers' here saved my life, you see.'

'He did?'

'I'd have been burned to death, but for him. It was all Steve Moran's work. He set the place on fire, with me in it.' Gloria settled herself in an armchair and concluded the story in comfort. When she had finished, 'Fingers' was grinning widely.

'Guess that makes your abduction charge blow up in your face, McArdel, doesn't it?' he asked.

'What it amounts to is you are working for 'Fingers' of your own free will?' McArdel asked quietly.

Gloria spread her hands. 'No reason why I shouldn't, is there? He's offered me a good job, and an apartment, in return for doing a high spot in his floor show. I've got to live, Captain. I might as well have this job as any other.'

'You're sticking your chin out, Miss Vane,' McArdel said. 'The only difference between Ace Monohan and 'Fingers' here, is that 'Fingers' has a smooth line, especially with women of your sort — and Ace hasn't. That's straight — and think it over. Now, to get back to business; do you realize you've run foul of the law in not reporting to me, or some police head-quarters, the moment you had returned to town? You must have known that there was a hunt going on for you.'

'I thought of it, but — ' Gloria hesitated. 'I didn't want to become involved. Since I was forced to string along with Ace, I didn't know whether or not the police thought me an accessory. So I kept quiet.'

'That angle's safe enough, McArdel,' 'Fingers' said. 'You can't do a thing. She works for me of her own free will, and I saved her life. What do you think you can do with that?'

'Nothing,' McArdel admitted. 'You got here before me, 'Fingers'. Ace, though, has a murder charge to face. Have you any idea where he might be found, Miss Vane?'

'Not the slightest. As I told you, he dashed off with Al and told me to follow him. I haven't seen or heard of him since.'

'You say that he went for you in a big way — that you played up to him to try to get him to spill some information about his haul. Do you think he cares enough about you to try and get in touch with you?'

'Perhaps. But he doesn't know where I am. He doesn't even know what happened to me after I failed to follow him.'

McArdel was silent. 'Fingers' stirred at the desk, doing his best not to look impatient.

'Time you went, McArdel, isn't it?' he asked bluntly. 'Your coffee'll be getting cold back at headquarters.'

McArdel looked at him, then at the girl.

'Watch your step, Miss Vane,' he said quietly. 'If you find yourself in trouble, get in touch with me.'

'After all, Captain, I'm not a child,' Gloria said, with a shrug.

'You're a woman, though — and I know 'Fingers'.'

With that, McArdel went, but his visit had not been quite so fruitless, after all. After he had returned to his office, he sat thinking things out for a while. Then he looked at Sergeant Clayton as he sat plugging out reports on a noiseless typewriter.

'Since Ace has ditched us for the time being, sergeant,' he said, 'our angle, I think, is to keep a watch on Gloria Vane.'

'How come, sir?'

'I gathered enough to realize that Miss Vane acts on Ace like a magnet. He doesn't know she hates the living sight of him and, for two reasons, I expect him to try and drift back into town — especially after that break away he made from that freight train. For one thing, Ace doesn't know what happened to Gloria, and that must be making him feel pretty sore — but he does know that 'Fingers' was the cause of all the trouble and, if I know Ace, he'll try and put the bead on 'Fingers'. If he does, it's possible he may find out at the same time that Gloria is alive — and well — and that will take him straight to her, and us to him. We'll keep alert, of course, but I think the issue boils down to Ace himself now.'

'And what about the rock pile he must be carrying around with him?'

'I imagine he'll just go on carrying it for the time being. He must have a fence in view, I suppose, but he won't be able to contact him as long as we keep him on the run. Yes, give him long enough, and he'll run straight into his own trap.'

After a moment's thought, the sergeant said: 'What do you suppose the Vane girl is driving at, sir? All she has done is exchange one gunman for another. Is she partial to them, or what?'

'I don't quite get her angle,' McArdel confessed. 'If there is one at all, I'd say she's fallen for 'Fingers' slick city ways, and sees no harm in giving herself a well-paid job and an apartment at 'Fingers' expense. She reasons — and probably rightly — that 'Fingers' can't be any worse than Ace was. That, I say, is how it looks. There may be more to it. I don't like the set-up, either. Miss Vane's a decent girl at heart, and I don't like to see her kicked around like this. I warned her as clearly as I could, without saying something 'Fingers' could pin me for.'

7

Ace got out of the river — and nobody saw him do it. In fact it was sheer luck, which, for once, was on his side. He knew, after swimming for nearly an hour in the moonlight, that he couldn't hold out much longer. He knew, also, that the distant black triangle sweeping through the water with its searchlight blazing was a police cutter.

Then he was dragged below surface by an irresistible current. With bursting lungs he was hurtled though a dark tunnel — some ancient culvert or other — at dizzying speed. Just as he felt sure it was curtains, he found himself flung clear and landed like a hooked fish on a massive steel grating, water pouring all around him, but no longer solid enough to drown him.

Dazed, bruised, panting hard, he got to his feet. He had by now gotten so accustomed to darkness that the starlight shining down through an infinitely long shaft overhead seemed almost bright. He was deep down in an underground sewer of some kind — and it wasn't poisonous, either. There was no smell — no anything, except the gurgle of water.

He moved. His footfalls on the iron grating echoed. In a moment or two, he had left the grating and went on his way down a black abyss of tunnel, his fingers stroking slime on the walls as he went.

Just whereabouts he was on the map, he had no idea. He had leapt into the river at the Pennsylvania-New Jersey border, and he knew no more than that. He might be going right back into Penn. for all he knew — or, as he hoped, heading under New Jersey in the general direction of New York. He was safe from the cops for the moment, anyway, and that was something.

But he was getting tired again — damned tired. His sleep in the freight train had been only brief, and he had gone through mighty exertions since. He would have settled there and then for a sleep, except for the fact that he had no idea whether or not a tidal flood of water might not overtake him. So he kept on going, through endless dark, amidst everlasting echoes.

His feet were dragging and he seemed to have gone a hundred miles before he realized the dark was lightening. It gave him new strength. He hurried on and came to another shaft curving up into remoteness. The stars had gone and it was daylight outside. Far over his head were the outlines of a grating and shadows hurrying across it. And something else — a rusty iron ladder driven into the side of the shaft. Distinctly, he heard the noise of a car. More shadows. Then a big black one, as something completely covered the opening and moved on again.

Weary though he was, he began climbing. Halfway up the shaft, he was plunged into semi-darkness again as the big grating became obliterated — and stayed that way. Puzzled, he kept on going up until he could get no higher. Squinting between the iron bars, he found himself looking at the underside of a big truck. He strained his eyes to the uttermost angle, but the truck blocked his view. He could not make out whether he was under a street, a goods yard, a loading station, or what the hell —

Voices. He listened intently.

'Okay, Bill — that's all for now.'

'You're full, anyway,' replied a man's voice cheerfully. 'Take her away.'

Suddenly, there was the blasting roar of a powerful motor engine and clouds of pungent gasoline fumes came billowing down into Ace's face. He watched the transmission axle on the truck spin, then the vehicle began moving and gave him a view of clear blue sky.

He angled forward again and, this time, on a diagonal slant, he could just see the top of a signboard — BILL'S PULL-IN GAS STATION. That satisfied him. He had come up under the runway of a filling station, probably one of those spots on the high road where the long-distance drivers pulled in for a bite, and a gas and oil check-over.

Ace thought. Seemed to be only one man running the joint. If it were possible to get out and hold him up with his gun

— He couldn't do more than scare the guy, because the water had ruined the automatic. Ace stopped thinking for a moment as there was a queer scraping sound coming nearer overhead. Presently, clouds of dust began to sift through the grid and rained down into his upturned face. He held his nose desperately, to stop himself from sneezing.

His eyes smarting, he glared above him as the dust subsided a little. The grating darkened and the man himself appeared — a spare guy, not very old, in greasy coveralls. From below, he was oddly foreshortened, his boot soles blocking out the light. Ace sized him up. Kind of guy he could take care of if there were not too many others, and if the grating was moveable. Have to wait his chance. Then he might frisk a car and make a dash for it to New York.

Another truck arrived a bit more to one side on the runway than the previous one. Ace watched the garage owner and the truck driver talking for a while, then moved on. At the same time an idea struck him. If he could find a truck high enough in wheelbase, he might somehow smuggle himself up under the chassis and stay there. Be a lousy ride, but it would get him on the move and out of sight.

He waited until things seemed reasonably clear above and then edged himself up by one rung. Clinging with one hand, he pushed on the grating with the other. It lifted fairly easily. He raised it perhaps half an inch, experimentally, then dropped it down again. When the chance came, he might be able to do something about it.

It was a long time coming. Trucks and private cars both came to fill up, but always seemed to be too much to one side of the grid for safety — as far as he was concerned. Then, just as he was commencing to think he would have to resort to his gun bluff after all, he got a break. There was a rushing sound overhead and, from his angle, he could see the sleek streamlining of a high-powered limousine. He expected a chauffeur to appear when the driving wheel door opened, but instead, it was the head and shoulders of a girl who came into sight, looking about her. She was dressed in some kind of summer frock — as far as Ace could tell, for the view was limited to her head and shoulders — and her hair was red and flowing. She looked a hot number, and she looked annoyed.

'Bill!' she shouted, making a megaphone of her hand to do so. 'Bill! Give me a bit of service here! I've got to make it to New York in a hurry!'

New York? Ace became more attentive. He saw the girl lean in the car and bang her hand on the electric horn button. It had an effect, for there came the running feet of Bill, and his apologetic voice.

'Sorry, Miss Drew, just finishing a job back there. How much gas?'

'Fill her up.'

His feet sounded as he went to a pump. The girl relaxed against the car and took out a compact, began to line in her lips gently. Yes, she was a good-looker, Ace decided. From his low angle, the bosomy effect she produced was intriguing.

'Going to New York, Miss Drew, did you say?' came Bill's voice.

'Uh-huh.' The girl tossed her compact back into the car. 'It isn't all hay, being a secretary-chauffeuse, sometimes. I get yanked off to all sorts of places without warning.'

Ace listened, and looked again. He could see enough of the limousine's window to realize the car was empty. She was going to New York. She was only a girl, and it wouldn't be difficult to make her take him as a passenger. But how to —

'That reminds me,' the girl said suddenly, and came forward a little. 'Any news on that locket I brought in? Get anything on it?'

'I'm doing my best with it. Miss Drew,' Bill's voice showed he was approaching. Ace saw her hand over some money: then Bill said: 'Want to see it now it's broken down?'

'Why not? I can take time for that.'

The girl walked forward with Bill beside her. Ace stared and whistled softly at the eyeful he got, then grim business knocked his momentary pleasure on the head, and he took the risk of pushing up the grating gently. The moment he did so, he saw the girl and Bill going into a workshop some little distance away on the other side of the runway. The glazed window prevented them from seeing out.

Ace wriggled free, pushed the grating back in place, then pulled quickly on the car's rear door. It moved. He slid inside, lay on the floor and, after latching the door, pulled a skin rug over him. Tugging out his gun, he lay half smothered, waiting.

He had not to wait long. The girl got into the car's driving seat and slammed the door. Bill's cheerful voice called goodbye to her; then the limousine was on the move. Ace sighed thankfully to himself and pushed away the skin rug somewhat. He knew the girl could not notice him with her attention concentrated on her driving, so he took time out to breathe more freely. The only thing that had him worried was whether the girl would pick anybody else up on the way — or whether a police block might stop her and make things difficult.

This unpleasant possibility grew on Ace. He eased himself a little higher and looked about him. Keeping dead behind the girl, so his reflection would not appear in the driving mirror, he peered at the front seat beside her. On it lay her topcoat, with the compact thrown on top of it. From the pocket of the coat, a silk choker was dangling. Ace grinned a little. He rose higher and put the muzzle of his gun dead between the girl's shoulder blades.

She started in alarm at the cold shock through her thin dress. She shot a glance at Ace through the mirror, then watched the empty main road down which she was speeding the car.

'You got yourself a passenger, baby,' Ace explained. 'And I mean business. One word the wrong way from you, and I'll let you have it neat, right in the spine. Get it?'

'I'm not a fool,' she said calmly. 'Of course I get it. Where did you get aboard, anyway?'

'Never mind.' Ace reached over and lifted the compact and coat. 'You got yourself a sick sister,' he said dryly. 'Just in case the police stop you.'

She said nothing, but Ace noticed her

frowning. He went into the corner of the rear seat and began to clean his face with his shirt cuff and then made himself up with the powder puff and lipstick. Excess of powder made his face suitably pale. Lipstick in the right shading gave him a look of high temperature. When he had the orange-colored kerchief draped around his head and ears, and the girl's coat on — the collar well pulled up — it would have been impossible to tell he was Ace — or even a man at all.

Satisfied with his appearance, he clambered into the front seat beside the girl and kept his gun pressed low down above the swelling line of her right hip.

'Pretty good,' she commented, shooting him a quick glance. 'Remind me to burn that coat when you've finished — and the choker, too.'

'Stop being funny, and remember I'm your sister. You're rushing me to New York to see a specialist. That's for the police, see? Try anything, and it'll be the finish.'

'I shan't,' she said. 'You can have a free ride if you want; it isn't my car, anyway.'

'I know that; you're secretary-driver to some big shot, ain't you?'

'Yes — Grantham Lord the New York share broker But how on earth did you know that?'

'I came up out of a hole. I was under that grid in Bill's runway.'

'Oh — I see.' The girl gave a start. 'You — you mean you heard me talking to Bill?'

'Yeah. I heard everything.'

She gave him an amused glance of her gray eyes. It puzzled him. Most dames he'd known would have gone purple with embarrassment.

'I thought you'd be sore about that,' he said. 'Anyway, it wasn't deliberate, me being down there. Just one of those things.'

She shrugged. 'I don't care much. You might as well have your fun while you can. You certainly won't when the police catch up on you — Ace!'

'You know me, huh?'

'Obviously. Your picture's in every paper, and there's a hunt in every hole and corner. But you needn't worry. I shan't spill anything if I'm stopped. I like taking chances, and I believe, in giving the other guy a break.'

'You talk my language, kid,' Ace murmured. 'Pity the heat's on, otherwise you an' me could ring doorbells.'

'If you ever beat the rap long enough to walk around free, Ace, you can always contact me at Bill's. He's a friend of mine. Does odd jobs, like selling lockets and things that have gotten lost.'

'Lost — or frisked?'

The girl smiled. 'Figure it out for yourself. I don't mean to stay a secretary-chauffeuse to a pot-belly all my life. I like cash on the side. Bill fixes it for me.'

'He's a fence,' Ace said, snapping his fingers. 'An' you an' me are in the same line of business.'

'On the side, yes,' she agreed. 'Now you know why I'm willing to take care of you till you hit New York.'

Ace relaxed inside the girl's coat and drew the choker, further round his face. He knew he was safe for the moment. He patted the girl's thigh as she sat beside him. She accepted it without even a glance.

* * *

Gloria had finished her act in the floorshow — her first night at the job — when the waiter told her the boss wanted to see her. She nodded and, amidst the glitter of sequins on her evening gown, made her way to the private stairway leading to 'Fingers'' office. She half expected she was going to be in bad trouble: she hadn't thought much of her effort on the floor, even if the customers had applauded loudly.

She found 'Fingers' smiling, however. He got up from his desk to greet her — immaculate in his tuxedo, as usual — and drew up a chair.

'Have a seat, honey,' he invited. 'And a cigarette.'

She accepted both. He lit the cigarette for her and put the lighter away slowly. Gloria waited. She liked the way his blond hair waved; she liked the — In fact, she just liked.

'I've been thinking,' he said. 'It looks as though Ace is still on the loose, doesn't it? No sign of him, having been caught, anyway, and there darned soon would be if he had.'

'What's your interest in Ace, outside the stolen stuff he's got?' Gloria asked.

'My interest in him is that he's dangerous as long as he's around.' 'Fingers' set his steel-trap mouth. 'You maybe haven't thought it out the same as I have. He must be mighty sore at me for breaking up your contact with him. One day, he might aim to take care of me on that account I don't fancy getting a slug in my back when I least expect it.'

Gloria said nothing. The smoke curled up from her cigarette as it hung between her fingers.

'I think.' 'Fingers' said, 'it might be a good idea if you let him know you're still alive.'

'I don't go for that idea.' Gloria answered. 'I got free of him and, after, the way he mauled me, I'm not aching to get back to him. Count me out.'

'No, baby, I'm not counting you out.'

There was an odd look in 'Fingers' pale blue eyes. 'You said when I took you over that I'd send in a bill later. You were right. This is it. I took you over because you're the one person on this earth who can help me put Ace where he belongs.'

'I'm glad to know why you became so friendly. I thought you wanted me for — other things.'

'Fingers' shook his head. 'I told you. Women, as such, don't mean a thing to me. I keep 'em out of my affairs as much as possible. They've all got two legs and a body, I guess — and that's all there is to it.'

Gloria's expression changed a little. She seemed to be doing a spell of thinking to herself.

'There's one sure thing,' 'Fingers' continued, 'Ace will be watching all the papers to see how things are going — and, since he was last seen on the New Jersey border, it's possible that one paper he'll pick, up is the 'New York Times'. There's no guarantee he'll read the 'Personal Column', but it's worth a gamble.'

'What do you want in it?' Gloria asked. ''All forgiven. Come home'?'

'Fingers' grinned a little. 'Not quite, but pretty close. I've worked it out properly. Here.' He reached to his desk and took up a sheet from his scratchpad. He read aloud what he had written: 'Alive and well. Must see you. Main entrance Grand Central station. Tuesday evening at seven. You still rate aces with me. Gloria.'

'Hmmm — he may understand it if he sees it,' Gloria admitted.

'He will. All that has to be done is for you to keep the appointment on Tuesday. Tomorrow, you'd better take the ad. yourself to the 'Times' offices, then everything will be genuine. When Ace tries to meet you, I'll be there with my boys, out of sight, of course. After that, you've done your job.'

'But it's a task for the police, surely?' Gloria demanded. 'Just what do you want to nab Ace for?'

'Obvious reasons,' 'Fingers' retorted. 'He's got the whale of a lot of sugar with him — or should have. If he hasn't, I'll

make him tell me where it is. You don't
suppose I'm having the cops in on that,
do you? They'll find Ace later, and if he's
then a stiff, it'll be just too bad.'

'You mean, you want me to be — the
bait? To get him to come and walk to his
death?'

'Put it that way if you like.' He looked
surprised. 'Just what's eatin' you, kid?
That's the way it is. Ace is overdue for a
ride anyway.'

'Maybe he is, but I don't see it has
anything to do with us — or, at least, with
me.'

'You crazy? He mussed you up plenty,
didn't he?'

'Yes, but — ' Gloria put her finger and
thumb to her eyes for a moment. 'It's just
that I — I don't like being the cause of his
death, even though he is a killer.'

'Fingers' smiled and gave her the note.
'Take this along in the morning, kid,
before you come here — and don't go
sappy over Ace. He deserves all that's
coming to him.'

Gloria took the note, got on her feet,
and beyond bidding 'Fingers' goodnight,

she said no more. She went home to her apartment, thinking lots of things — things that kept her awake half the night. By the time morning had come, she had reached a decision. When she left her apartment she did not go direct to the 'Times' office. Instead, she went to police headquarters and got herself an interview with Captain McArdel.

'Well, Miss Vane, has trouble started?' he asked her dryly, when she was seated. 'You can't say I didn't warn you.'

'No trouble of the kind you mean, Captain, but a situation has come up which I think you should know about. It puts me in a position which scares me.'

He waited, then took the sheet from the scratchpad which she handed him. He raised his brows as he read it.

'Your idea?' he enquired.

'No — 'Fingers''. I'm the catspaw. I've to put that ad, in the 'Times', meet Ace — if he shows up — and 'Fingers' will do the rest. That's what I don't like. Apart from the fact that Ace's capture is solely a police job, I don't want to be the instrument by which Ace is decoyed to his death — and maybe torture. 'Fingers' says he'll make Ace talk about those jewels he stole.'

'And 'Fingers' will!' McArdel confirmed; 'I know him only too well. May sound odd to you, Miss Vane — but of the two men, I'd give Ace a break before I'd give 'Fingers' one. He's inhuman. Ace is a killer, sure, but an impulsive one. He's no sadist.'

'I — I've learned quite a deal about 'Fingers',' Gloria said slowly, thinking.

'Uh-huh? So soon?'

'Not in quite the way I'd expected.' Gloria gave a direct look. 'I suppose you wondered why I completely attached myself to 'Fingers' after the way I'd been treated by Ace?'

'I wondered, yes, but it's none of my business. You are a free agent.'

'I did it for a double reason — or even a three-fold one, come to that. First, I knew that if I stayed beside 'Fingers', I was safe from Ace's beastly mauling; second — my money was running out, and I needed well-paid work and an apartment; and thirdly, I fell for 'Fingers'.'

'Fell for him?' McArdel repeated blankly.

'That's what I said. He got me, somehow. Just my type, with that friendly grin and blond hair. I thought I was well away, and the fact that he had a doubtful reputation didn't bother me in the least. I thought that when he'd seen more of me — literally — he and I could go double-harness.' Gloria gave a wistful smile. 'Queer, that! Ace just wouldn't let me alone when he saw how much I'd got in the way of feminine charm; while 'Fingers' just looks at me like an iceberg and says I'm like all women — I just have two legs and a body. It's infuriating. If you were a woman, you'd know just how infuriating.'

McArdel shrugged. 'Afraid that's a personal problem, Miss. Vane. All I can tell you is that you'd be better away from 'Fingers', this town, and this State. He's dynamite.'

'It was only last night I realized how little he thinks of me,' Gloria continued. 'He took me under his wing purely so I could lead him to Ace. I'm not going to do it. I don't see why I should give 'Fingers' a break — and I don't want to decoy any man to his death, even if he is a killer. It's not my job. So, what do you think I should do?'

McArdel handed her the scratchpad sheet.

'Put this in the 'Times' as you've been told. I'll do the rest. Naturally if you value your life, you'll not say anything to 'Fingers'.'

'Yes, but what happens when he finds out that you've turned up and spoiled his game?'

'You don't have to worry, Miss Vane. When we take care of Ace, we'll also take care of 'Fingers'. For long enough, I've been wanting to pick up those two guys together, chiefly because one will tell on the other. In this case, Ace has enough loaded against him to get the death sentence, but 'Fingers' has managed to keep his nose clean. Ace knows plenty about him, though, and I'll very soon find a charge that will stick when Ace starts talking. However, that's my worry. You just go on as though nothing had happened. When 'Fingers' and Ace are out of the way, you can decide then what to do.'

'Thanks, Captain,' Gloria said gratefully, rising and shaking hands. 'And — and I hope you haven't got me down as a girl who isn't too particular?'

'Would it matter if I had?' he asked dryly; and, since she could think of no answer to this one, Gloria left the office. McArdel looked across at Sergeant Clayton as he worked in his corner.

'Funny, when you think of it,' Clayton said. 'Just shows you can't weigh up women, either. When they get a guy who nearly takes 'em apart, they don't like it; and when they get a guy who doesn't bat an eyelid, they blow up. What do they want?'

'Want me to answer that?' McArdel enquired, and he returned to his desk.

8

As she left headquarters and returned to the main street, Gloria was surprised to find a hand suddenly close round her upper arm. She made to drag free, then paused in surprise. The man holding her was Toni, head waiter at the 'Silver Slipper'.

'Well — why so attentive?' she asked, continuing to walk on.

'Just my job,' he replied. 'I'm not just a head waiter, sweetheart; I'm also strong-arm man for 'Fingers'. That means I tail anybody he asks — like I tailed you.'

Gloria gave a start. 'You mean you — you saw me go — '

'I saw you go home last night. A guy took over in the night and kept watch. I returned at dawn. I saw you leave. I saw you go to police headquarters — an' that's one place the boss just doesn't like. Before you do anything else, you'd better explain why you went to see McArdel.

But don't explain, to me. I'm not interested — but the boss will be.'

Gloria gave a helpless glance about her, but there was nothing she could do. Toni had a steel grip upon her, and he kept it there until he had led her into 'Fingers'' office. Then he released her, cuffed up his hat on to his forehead, and stood with his broad back to the door.

'What gives?' 'Fingers' asked, looking up from his desk in surprise.

Toni told him. Gloria stood watching 'Fingers'' steel-trap mouth set into a straight line. He got up from his swivel chair and came over to her.

'What did you tell McArdel?' he asked deliberately.

'All that I thought he should know!' Gloria retorted calmly, her smoke-gray eyes defiant.

'Yeah? — and after me telling you we didn't want the cops in on things? I don't like little girls who step outa line, Gloria. I can guess exactly what you spilled — all about the advertisement to bait Ace, huh?'

Gloria said nothing 'Fingers' looked at

her stonily, then glanced at Toni

'Did she go to the 'Times' office?'

'No, boss. Went straight to McArdel from her apartment. Maybe she figgered on going to the 'Times' when she left headquarters, but I didn't give her the chance.'

'Okay. That's all from you, Toni. You can blow.'

Toni went and the door closed. 'Fingers' strolled over to it and turned the key in the lock. He came back almost leisurely to where Gloria was standing and began to study her fixedly. 'I'll take care of that ad.,' he said, holding out his hand. 'Now you've spilled everything to the cops it isn't worth putting in the paper. Hand it over.'

Gloria took it from her handbag and gave it to him.

'You've cheated me out of bringing Ace here and getting him to speak about his rock-pile,' he said, balling the paper up in his hand. 'I don't like that, see? It's upset everything I've planned to do. As I told you, little girls shouldn't get outa line — '

With devastating speed, his right hand

came up and struck her across the face with such violence that she twisted sideways and dropped heavily to the carpet. What happened after that she was not quite sure. Her shoulder was seized and she was dragged on her feet, only to receive a blow in the mouth that felt as though it had smashed out her front teeth.

Her tongue salty, she collapsed across the desk, her clutching fingers on the big, heavy, silver inkpot. She lifted it up, the ink swilling across the desk and then over her two-piece. She had no chance to land it. The merciless fist was there again, slamming her clean across the desk so she collapsed helplessly on the other hide.

Dazed, blood trickling from the corner of her mouth, she tried to get on to her knees. She saw 'Fingers' coming towards her. His hand descended, twisted into her mass of thick blonde hair and dragged her to her feet. Panting desperately, she gazed into his merciless face. He was smiling frozenly.

'You're low down,' he whispered. 'Like all women. Never can trust 'em. Give 'em the least chance, and they'll stab you for sure — right in the back. But you'll learn, sister,' he added, shaking her head so violently the room seemed to spin. 'You'll learn never to go back on me again.'

He released her hair and she swayed drunkenly. She could not think straight. Her mouth and head were aflame with pain from the murderous punches she had received. 'Fingers' contemplated her and then stooped and swung her over his shoulder. She kicked feebly and uselessly as he carried her into the small room adjoining his office. In here were filing cabinets and other office requisites.

He set her on her feet and she whimpered a little, wiping the blood stupidly from the corner of her mouth, her hair sweeping down across her battered face.

'See that?' 'Fingers' snapped, and pointed to a massive pulley in the ceiling from which a strong rope was hanging. 'That's my persuader-and-punisher. Plenty of guys, and women too, who've tried to cross me have been given a work-over in here, and on that rope! If you ever try and double-cross me again, you'll get yourself strung up by the heels. Get it?'

Gloria remained swaying slightly supporting herself against a filing cabinet. Quite by accident, she found the cabinet door was unlocked. Her hands behind her, she was gripping the door's handle to support herself. She looked at 'Fingers' malevolently through her tangle of hair.

'McArdel was right,' she muttered, speaking with difficulty. 'He said you were a sadist, but that was an understatement. Any guy who'll punish a woman like you've done wants a bullet in his brain, and the quicker the better, you low-down, filthy swine!' she finished in a shriek, and whirled open the steel cabinet door with all her strength.

As she intended, it battered straight into 'Fingers'' sardonic face and set him stumbling backwards with a gasp. He clawed at the next cabinet and saved himself from falling. Gloria spun round and dived for the door — with some difficulty, for she was still half stunned.

She had only just got into the main office when 'Fingers' caught up with her.

She lashed out at him with her nails, gouging deep slashes down his face. He winced and yelped with sudden pain. She lashed again, straight at his eyes — and missed. Instead, the nail of her index finger, overlong, dug into his lip and split it.

'You thrice damned little hellcat!' he swore. 'Not satisfied with a double-cross, you hafta dig pieces out of me. I'll show you! You can't do that sort of thing to me an' get away with it. No blasted dame can!'

He dived for her as she tore away from him. The brief distance between him and her gave her the chance to spin round. As she did so, she saw him coming. Her foot shot up and kicked him straight in the stomach. He doubled up, his breath escaping in an explosive gasp — but he held on to her foot savagely and slammed her over on to her back.

She wrenched savagely, and her shoe came off in his grip. Reaching out her hand, she seized the steel waste-paper basket and battered it relentlessly against his head as he still remained half doubled up, cursing the agony in his stomach. He half straightened and put up his hands to protect his head. He seized the waste-paper basket as it came round again and wrenched it from her.

She half wriggled away along the floor, reaching out for the massive inkpot that she had dropped earlier on. He was upon her almost immediately, gripping her wrists and forcing them back and up until she screamed with the pain. Holding her thus, he dragged her back along the floor towards the little office.

What his intention was, Gloria did not know, and was nearly too dizzy to care. But she still had one trick to play and, being an acrobatic dancer among other things, it stood a chance of success. At the moment, she was face downwards, her arms dragged up as he pulled her along. She waited until he had pulled her into the little office and stopped moving. Apparently, he was doing something to the rope hanging over the pulley and, to do it, he had to release her right arm.

That was all she needed. She put her right palm flat on the floor, tensed herself, then with the ease of long training as an acrobatic dancer, she stood on her head, at the same time lashing her feet over and backwards.

Her sudden inversion dragged 'Fingers' down towards her as he held her wrist. Two things happened — as she'd calculated. He had to release her and, simultaneously, her feet struck him a blinding blow clean in the face. One of her feet had a shoe on, the other none. The one with the shoe did the trick. With all her weight behind the impact, 'Fingers' just did not know what hit him. Fire exploded behind his eyes, and he toppled backward on his heels, hitting the edge of the open cabinet door as he went. He became motionless, pole-axed — blood trickling from his nose.

Gloria overbalanced backwards and fell heavily on top of him. For a moment or two, she was too exhausted to move; then she felt something metallic pressing into her from one of his pockets. On impulse she dived her hand in, and it came out with his car keys. She got to her feet drunkenly. Aching and twinging from a myriad bruises, she clawed her way into the main office and dragged on her shoe. Then she stood thinking for a moment. At length she went over to the little office door and shut it, turning the key in the lock. She would have liked to have hanged 'Fingers' by the heels, as he had sworn to do to her if she ever double-crossed him again, but his weight was too much for her. So she let him be Meantime, she had to get out.

To go through the building was impossible in her appalling condition — but there was the fire escape outside the window. She took a drink of water from the cooler, winced as the fluid went over her smashed teeth and damaged lips, then she staggered to the window and raised it. All was clear in the alley below, and 'Fingers'' own sedan was parked there as usual.

She made up her mind. Picking up her handbag, she put 'Fingers'' car keys in it, then began an unsteady descent of the fire escape. By the time she had got down to the car, she was feeling less rocky. She got into it and, keeping her head down as much as possible to avoid drawing attention to her face, she drove through the back streets until she had reached the office of the 'New York Times'.

Drawing the car in to the kerb, she hesitated for a moment, then decided to carry through her plan. She got out of the car and, ignoring the amazed looks of passers-by, went into the main entrance-way of the building.

Almost immediately a commissionaire stood in front of her.

'Madam, what in — ?' He stopped, lost for words.

'I want the city editor,' she said urgently. 'I must see him. I've got a story for him; that's why I'm in this awful mess.'

News being the life-blood of a daily, the commissionaire found a quiet way to get her into the city editor's office. He sat staring at her blankly as she half reeled in.

'Holy cat!' he exclaimed, and got quickly on his feet. 'What in Sam Hill happened to you, lady?'

He caught her in his arms as she swayed. Drawing up a chair he settled her in it. She revived a little as he handed her a drink. He stood watching her as she swallowed the water painfully. In all his experience, no woman in such a state had ever walked into his sanctum. Her face was bulging in three places from livid bruises, and blood smears were across her forehead and chin. Three of her upper front teeth were missing. Her hair was tumbled and matted, but still retained traces of waves. Her skirt had ripped halfway up her thigh, and the gray jacket she had been wearing had gone altogether. Instead, there was her white silk blouse, ripped away from one shoulder and the collar hanging by a thread. From the end of one short sleeve; the loops of a shoulder strap hung.

'Take a look at me,' she breathed, crushing up the cardboard water carton and throwing it in the waste-paper basket. 'I'm Gloria Vane.'

'You're — ' The city editor came closer and began to whistle. 'The girl who was abducted by Ace Monohan, and then went over to 'Fingers' Baxter you mean? Yeah, I heard about that from the police.'

'Fingers did this to me,' she went on venomously. ' 'Fingers'! I was willing to do anything for him. I thought we were going to be friends — then, when I suggested we get together, he pitched into me! For no reason. The dirty sadist, he beat the tar out of me! You can see it for yourself!'

'Yeah, yeah — sure I can!' the city editor said.

'He threatened to kill me, but I got out just in time. This is a story, isn't it? 'Fingers', the slick guy, treats his girl friend like this! And for no reason! Just so as to be tough!'

She put a hand to her forehead for a moment and sank back in her chair. Then she steadied again.

'It's time folk knew the way 'Fingers' behaves, isn't it?' she demanded. 'I'm entitled to let everybody see what he's done to me, aren't I?'

The editor made some notes and pressed a bell push.

'Lady I've wanted a chance for years to pin something on 'Fingers' and this story of yours is a lulu. It won't get him in jail, because there's only your word for it that he did it — but it's good enough for me. I'll have your picture, if you don't mind — just as you are.'

'That's how I want it.' Gloria said, her eyes gleaming — then she looked up as a photographer came in.

In a few moments his flashbulb had glared three times and she had been transferred to the plates. She held on to the edge of the desk for support and looked at the editor.

'I don't want paying for this,' she said. 'I just want a good exposé of 'Fingers'.'

'There'll be one, Miss Vane — and you'll get paid, because the law says you must. Now, how's about you seeing a doctor, or my calling an ambulance?'

She shook her head. 'I'm going to my apartment — 479a, Pembroke Building, Fifty-ninth Street. I'll put myself right. You can send your check there. All I want is to make that dirty swine 'Fingers' smart.'

'I don't know about that,' the city editor said, 'but he certainly won't like what I'm going to say. I'm giving this a banner headline. I never saw a woman so beaten up before. Why don't you go to the police and charge him with assault?'

'Because, as you said, there's only my word for it — and 'Fingers' knows all the legal tricks. No — I'll be satisfied with everybody knowing what he did to me.' Gloria picked up her handbag and put a hand to her aching mouth. 'I'll be going,' she added. 'The moment I'm cleaned up and, can move about again, I'd better go and get my teeth fixed.'

'I'll have the commissionaire show you the quietest way out,' the city editor said, and pressed the switch on his desk-phone.

★ ★ ★

Gloria reached her apartment in much the same way as she had escaped from 'Fingers'' office — via the fire escape, leaving his sedan at the back of the apartment building for the time being. That he would come chasing after her, she had little doubt, so for that reason she set about protecting herself before she made any attempt to patch herself up.

Picking up the phone, she got through to Captain McArdel. He listened in silence to all she had to say. When he did speak, his voice was both grim and yet, somehow, sympathetic.

'Afraid I warned you what you might get, Miss Vane — though I didn't expect it to be quite so soon. So the advertisement is off, and we're right back where we started?'

'The advertisement is off, Captain, but we've got something far better, than a chancy personal ad. At eight tonight, tomorrow's 'New York Times' will be on the stands, with headlines about me. Even to my photograph. Don't you see what that may mean? Ace is almost certain to see it, and he'll come rushing over from wherever he is to pay 'Fingers' out. That's why I told the city editor everything, though I didn't tell him 'Fingers' real reason for beating me up.'

'You've taken the devil of a risk, Miss Vane,' the police Captain said, seriously. 'When 'Fingers' sees those headlines, he's liable to do just anything to you.'

'I'll risk that, if only for revenge. The way I'm looking at it right now, Captain, one of two things can happen. Ace will perhaps try to reach me — which will be your chance to nail him if you want to; and 'Fingers' may also try and get at me. You'll then have both men at once — or should have 'Fingers' will know that those headlines are liable to bring Ace running, and he'll be waiting for him. It's up to you to watch how things work out, and strike as you think fit. This way, I don't feel I'm baiting Ace, as I would have been with that ad. I want to bring him into the open so you can get at him, and I also want 'Fingers' nailed too, somehow, for the hell he's given me. That clear enough?'

'Clear enough,' McArdel agreed. 'We'll keep tabs on everything that happens, don't you worry. Neither Ace nor 'Fingers' will get far without me knowing all about it.'

McArdel rang off and Gloria put the phone down. She gave a little sigh of relief and then wandered into the bathroom and began the job of patching herself up. A warm shower, the application of ointment, and a change to pyjamas and negligée, made her feel somewhat better. Her mouth still kept hurting abominably and it looked atrocious, but that was something she would have to tolerate for the moment. When all her bruises had subsided sufficiently, she was resolved to find a dentist and get herself fixed with new teeth. She was satisfied that she had done all she could for the moment — and only McArdel and the city editor knew what her actions had been. The telephone line to police headquarters would certainly not be tapped.

Gloria gave 'Fingers'' parked sedan some thought. In the end, she decided to leave it where it was. If he came after it, or sent one of his boys to get it, it would hardly matter very much — and if police were around, they would probably take care of anybody who tried to take the car away. All in all, Gloria felt she could consider herself reasonably safe.

The morning passed and, at the end of it, she felt a good deal better. She had some lunch, then went to bed to await whatever developments there might be. It was also around lunchtime when 'Fingers' got himself released from his sub-office. It was Toni who let him out attracted at last by the puzzling remote bumping sounds from his boss's office.

''bout damned time!' was 'Fingers'' savage greeting, as he emerged into his main office and saw Toni staring at him in wonder. 'I thought you were all damned-well dead! I've been stuck in there since that bitch Gloria locked me in!'

'The dame?' Toni stared even more. 'You kiddin', boss? You mean she did this to you?'

'That's just what I mean. Where is she? What happened to her?'

'I ain't seen her — not since I showed her in here.'

'Fingers' looked about him, then at the open window. He didn't need to look any further. Muttering to himself, he snatched up a hand mirror from a drawer in his desk and inspected himself. He was not a pretty sight. The girl's nails had left three deep, vicious scratches across his face and his cut lip was swollen and puffy.

'Looks like you took it on the chin, boss,' Toni observed.

'Shut up! Think yourself lucky I don't kick your teeth in for lettin' that dame get away. She used the fire escape and, right now, I guess she'll be at her apartment, laughing about it all.'

'Unless she's blown town.'

'Not in the mess she was in. Take a bit to heal up — same as it will me.' 'Fingers' clenched his fist. 'I'm going to make her smart for this, Toni, later. First, I'm going to get myself put as near right as possible. I'll be back after lunch, if anybody wants me.'

Only just managing to keep his temper, he departed. With his handkerchief over his face, he went to the hairdresser's further down the road and ordered himself a warm pack. His personal appearance was a strong point with him; he couldn't afford to be around with the marks of a woman's nails across his face.

The more he thought about Gloria, the more he was fuming. He had discovered the theft of his car — and keys. He thought of all sorts of ways in which to deal with her — but gradually he began to cool off and considered the problem more dispassionately. She was his sworn enemy from now on, of course; he realized that; but she was also still the only person who could possibly enable him to get hold of Ace. That made it necessary to do a lot of things.

When 'Fingers' emerged from the hot towels, he had made up his mind. He would visit Gloria later and apologize. Even go on his knees and give her a fat check, if it would help. He just could not let her go her own way when she was so useful. But, once he had his mitts on Ace — ! From that instant onwards, she would count for less than nothing, and he could really give her the works.

And in the early evening, after a day in which both Gloria and Ace had been resting themselves, the 'New York Times' first edition the following day came on the streets and stands. It did not take 'Fingers' above ten minutes to discover the news. It leapt right out of the headlines and hit him as he mooched about his own office, trying to compose himself for the evening's business. He wondered why Toni — in his stiff shirt front — had been so mysteriously silent when he had brought in the paper. Now he knew.

'FINGERS" GIRL FRIEND TAKES IT ON THE LAMP!

'Fingers' sat down slowly, staring at the paper in fascination. Then he looked at the photograph of the battered girl. He read the columns of type, trying to absorb the slashing indictment that had been written about him. When he had come to the end of learning what a two-cent bum he was, he put the paper down and reflected. He was not furious; not even annoyed. It was not the first time newspapers had attacked him and stayed just inside the libel limits with the things they said.

It was the deeper issues that interested him. The fact that Gloria had apparently not mentioned the real reason for him beating her up. It didn't take him long to size up the angle.

'Pretty,' he murmured. 'Damned pretty!

She hopes that Ace will see this and come gunning for me — as he probably will. I couldn't like the set-up better. I don't have to apologize to Gloria. I don't have to do anything but sit here and wait for Ace to come to me — as he surely will. Yeah, I guess she's played right into my hands. In getting Ace to come looking for me, she's sending him right where I want him. All she needs now is to be left alone — then, after I've taken care of Ace, I can fix her — but good!'

He nodded to himself and took his automatic from the drawer. He was ready for action the moment Ace chose to show up.

9

Captain McArdel had also summed up the possibilities in pretty much the same way. It seemed logical to him that the first move Ace would make would be to tackle 'Fingers' — not only to avenge the manhandling of the girl, but also to find out from him where she was. Ignorant of her address, there was no other move Ace could make — or so McArdel figured. So he had his men keep a watch on the 'Silver Slipper'. Part of the shadows, they remained alert as the June evening deepened into night, and the lights of the night spot came up brightly.

Apparently there was no sign of Ace — or of any character who might have seen him. Only the usual night spot habitués.

What both 'Fingers' and McArdel had overlooked however was that Ace was no fool. He saw the paper, and the headline, in the safety of an underworld dive where he had an army of friends to keep him from the heat. At first, he had gone off into a rave, then he had thought further. Accustomed to treading warily, it hadn't taken him long to decide that the whole thing might be a trick. To go off half-cocked might nail him with the cops for keeps.

So he figured out a new plan, and towards one in the morning, he was quite near the 'Silver Slipper', still in the midst of its night's business. He couldn't see anybody either near the front or back of the building, but that didn't deceive him. The cops had a way of looking like shadows, so nobody could tell the difference. In any case, it didn't matter much. He had no intention of moving from this spot — a deeply gloom-ridden recess in the wall at the corner of the main street and the alleyway, which led past the side of the 'Silver Slipper.'

Shortly, if the plan had worked, he would be picked up in a limousine owned by Grantham Lord, stockbroker, and driven by a girl who didn't much care for her morals. Indeed, Ace had seen quite a lot of Anna Drew since she had driven him safely into New York. He knew practically everything about her, enough to feel sure she'd help him in any scheme he suggested. He had had to give her some of his stolen jewelry in payment, of course, but he had considered it worth it. Right now, she was an essential factor in the plan.

And because she was loyal to Ace and, in a roundabout sort of way, fond of him, Anna drew up in the limousine at one-fifteen and then went past the commissionaire into the 'Silver Slipper's' main hall. The commissionaire looked after her in some puzzlement, wondering whether he ought to tell her she couldn't leave the car out front; then he judged, from her slacks, jacket and uniform cap that she was a chauffeuse, looking for somebody.

He followed her into the main hall as she gazed about her.

'Any help, miss?' he enquired.

'Pardon? Oh — yes.' She turned to him, smiling.

'I'm looking for the head waiter — '

'Toni?'

'I only know him as Mr. Carlotti. I have a message for him.'

The commissionaire nodded and told her to wait. She smiled to herself. So far, so good. This whole scheme being worked at two in the morning gave her free scope. Her boss was packed away in slumber in his Fifth Avenue penthouse, quite unaware of the strange private life of his Girl Friday.

Then, presently, Toni appeared in his crackling shirtfront. He looked at the girl in surprise.

'Yes, miss?' He spoke properly, with a great deal of difficulty, he much preferred his off-duty slang.

'I don't know whether you know me or not, Mr. Carlotti,' Anna said, 'But you do know Mr. Lord — the stockbroker. I've brought him here in the car many a time.'

'Sure — Grantham Lord. What about him?'

'He asked me to come here for you. He's got some kind of an important enquiry he wants you to put — concerning somebody who comes here quite a lot. I don't know the details, of course — but I do know the matter's urgent, and if you could spare half an hour, he'd like to talk to you.'

Toni reflected. 'Why didn't he come here?'

'He can't. His lumbago's acting up again. You'll have to go to him. I've got the car outside; I can run you straight over.'

The possibility that Toni might ring back to Lord and check on the invitation had already occurred to Anna. For that reason, she kept straight on talking and hoped she sounded convincing. Evidently she did, for Toni finally nodded.

'Okay — I don't see why not. I'll just fix it so my deputy can take over.'

'Suppose your boss won't let you, come?' Anna asked, and Toni grinned.

'He won't know. I make my own laws down here. He's in his office, and I'll be back before he knows it.'

He went off, to return in a few minutes in hat and overcoat. He accompanied the girl out to the limousine and stepped into it as she held the door open for him.

Before she could get into the driving seat, however, a figure in soft hat and mackintosh loomed up.

'Evening, miss. Your car?'

Anna straightened in surprise. 'Do I look as though I owned it? I only drive it. I'm Grantham Lord's chauffeuse.'

'Uh-huh. Mind if I look the car over?' The man displayed his authority card and then opened the back door. 'If you wouldn't mind stepping out a moment, Mr. Carlotti?'

Toni got out, wondering. He looked at the girl, and she gave a shrug. Thoroughly, the plainclothes man searched the rear of the car, and particularly behind the back seat, where there was ample room for anybody to hide. Anna thanked her stars that Ace had not decided to conceal himself, but had planned to be picked up later.

'Just what is all this about?' Anna demanded, as the plainclothes man finally withdrew to the sidewalk again.

'Safeguard,' he said laconically. 'Protecting you, Mr. Carlotti, if you must know. We're watching for a guy who might try to use you.'

'Meaning Ace Monohan?' Toni asked. 'Y' don't have to worry. I can take care of myself.'

He climbed back into the cushions and slammed the door. Anna settled herself at the steering wheel and sped the car down the quiet street. When it was safe, she turned right suddenly, and down a side road. Then, gradually, she began to drive back on her tracks, but to the far rear of the main road.

'I thought Mr. Lord lived in Fifth Avenue?' Toni said, looking intently outside. 'Where are you going?'

'Mr. Lord's at a nursing home,' Anna said, thinking up an excuse mighty fast. 'I told you he had lumbago.'

Toni said nothing, but he frowned to himself. He frowned even more when the girl slowed down as she passed a corner. Things happened so fast that Toni could not grasp them. The rear door shot open and shut again, then a figure in a soft hat and overcoat was beside him, a, glinting automatic in his hand.

'Keep goin' kid,' Ace instructed.

'You've done a swell job so far.'

'And only just,' Anna told him. 'The cops have been snooping around — but they got nowhere.'

'What gives?' Toni demanded, raising his hands a little as the gun jabbed at him.

'I don't have to tell you I'm Ace, do I?' Ace said, in a snarling tone. 'I want some information from you, fella — and I want it quick! I picked you 'cos you're closer to that dirty rat 'Fingers' than anybody else. And I want to know — where's Gloria Vane?'

'If you think I — ' Toni broke off his eyes watering as he got a violent slap across the face.

'I do think!' Ace grated. 'An' I'm not pullin' my punches, Toni. Where's Gloria?'

'I can't squeal on the boss, Ace! You know that, don't you — '

'You'll squeal an' like it!' Ace brought up his fist this time and jammed it relentlessly back and forth across Toni's face. He tried ineffectually to protect himself, and finally fell back amongst the cushions, breathing hard.

'Any more?' Ace demanded. 'I can keep this up longer than you can, brother!'

'Okay — okay!' Toni panted. 'I'm not so dumb I don't know when I'm licked. The dame's at 479a, Pembroke Buildings, Fifty-ninth. Unless she's moved. That is one of the joints 'Fingers' owns. The dame's got an apartment there.'

'Hear that, kid?' Ace asked the girl and as she nodded and drove on, he added: 'Go there — an' if it's right, we'll get rid of this mug. If it isn't, he'll talk further.'

'It's on the level, Ace,' Toni said, fingering his jaw.

'For your sake, brother, it had better be!'

Ace said no more. He watched intently as the girl swung the big car swiftly round corners and sped down innumerable streets, until at last she stopped a quarter of a mile from Pembroke Buildings on Fifty-ninth.

'Okay,' Ace said. 'Got your hardware, Anna?'

'Uh-huh.' She brought out a .32 from the cubbyhole and it glinted in the dashboard light. 'You go ahead, Ace. I can take care of this mug for as long as need be.'

'I'll find out first if she's there,' Ace said 'That is, if she's got a phone. She should have, in a joint like that.'

'She has,' Toni said, anxious to escape from the predicament he was in. 'Circle, four-nine-seven-six.'

Ace nodded and got out of the car. Aware that the apartment house might be covered by the police, he went away from it until he came to a phone kiosk. After a moment or two, to his profound satisfaction, the voice of Gloria spoke. He wondered at the slight lisp occasioned by her missing front teeth, and put it down to the line.

'Hello?' she asked, and paused. 'Hello? Who is this, please?'

As Ace remained silent, she spoke again. 'Hello? Gloria Vane speaking. Who's on the line?'

Ace rang off. He had no intention of revealing who he was. For all he knew, there might even be police in the girl's apartment, parked there, waiting for him. Far better to case the joint first. So he returned to the car where the girl still held Toni at the business end of her gun.

'Well?' Toni asked urgently. 'I was right, wasn't I? Did y'get her?'

'Yeah — you gave it me straight,' Ace agreed. 'What floor's she on?'

'Top. Apartment twenty-seven.'

'Which side of the building?'

'Left, overlooking that car park.'

Ace looked upwards towards the apartment house, and for a moment Anna forgot and looked with him. Instantly, Toni's hand lashed out and seized the gun from her. He slipped out of the already open door and turned the weapon on Ace.

'Okay,' Toni breathed. 'So it's my turn now. You are coming back with me to see the boss, Ace. That's the one thing he's waiting for — '

He got no further. Anna jammed her hand on the electric horn, and its sudden blast made Toni jump. Anna, knowing what was coming, was steeled to any shocks and slammed open her own door. It struck Toni violently and knocked the automatic flying. Ace had it instantly;

then he put it away as he caught sight of a cop on his beat advancing slowly from the distance.

'Beat it,' he said briefly to the girl. 'Never mind this guy. He's no love for cops, anyway. I'll see you again.'

Anna nodded and swept the limousine from the kerb, as Ace slammed the doors. The dazed Toni looked about him — saw the cop in one direction and Ace vanishing quickly towards a side alley in the other. Toni did not wait. As Ace had remarked, he had no liking for the law in any form whatsoever.

Ace slowed down when he considered he had put a safe distance between himself and the cop. Then he began to make his way back towards the apartment house. When he had reached the car park, he stood looking about its dim emptiness. As far as he could see, there was nobody on the watch — but, anyway, he didn't intend to risk it. He knew the girl's apartment was on the top floor and, for the moment, that was all that signified.

He investigated until he found a fire escape. Pulling down its lower section, he climbed it with silent speed until he had gained nearly the summit of the building. As he went, he peered in through windows and saw nothing interesting — until he came to the last window of all, at the highest point.

He had intended to go on to the roof, find a skylight, and enter the building that way; but now it was not necessary. He was looking through flimsy curtains right at Gloria as she sat under a reading lamp browsing through a novel. Not very earnestly, either, for she kept glancing about her.

Ace grinned and knocked on the glass. Instantly, the girl was on her feet, startled. What satisfied Ace was the gun she was now holding. That meant there were no police with her. She would not have been allowed to have it if there had been.

She backed away from the window, holding the gun as she went. Ace reached out and kicked the glass in with his foot. She did not fire, evidently waiting to see who the intruder was. Ace kept back out of range and called to her:

'It's me, honey — Ace! Put that hardware away.'

She hesitated and came forward again. Ace took a risk and showed himself. Gloria still did not fire as he reached inside the frame, snapped back the catch, and then pushed the frame up. In another moment he had stepped into the room and was at her side. Immediately he took the gun from her.

He didn't give her any chance to say anything. He seized her in a steel embrace and kissed her fiercely. Even if she had wanted to resist, she could not. His arms pinned her own to her sides. She could have shot him in the back had she wanted — but she didn't, for two reasons. For one thing, she was no killer, and, for another, her only objective as far as Ace was concerned was to hand him over to those who'd know how to deal with him — the police. She had promised McArdel she would, therefore —

She winced as Ace kissed her on the lips; then he drew back and held her at arm's length, studying her.

'Yeah, he sure beat you up, kid,' he

breathed. 'It won't be long now before I take care of 'Fingers' for what he's done — even knocked your teeth out, huh?'

'Uh-huh,' Gloria assented. 'But I can get those fixed later. What happened to you? How did you manage to get here?'

'I got here, didn't I? That's all that matters. You an' me, see? There never was anything else. Say, this is some joint!'

Gloria nodded slowly and cast an anxious look in the direction of the telephone. If she could only advise McArdel that Ace was here for the taking — unless he already knew.

'Anybody see you come here?' she asked.

'I guess not. What police there are seem to be stuck around 'Fingers' joint, mebbe thinking that I might show up an' take care of 'Fingers' for what he's done to you. Only I was smart, see? I kept outa sight, found out where you were, and came right over. Now, how about a drink?'

'Yes. Yes — of course.'

Gloria moved over to the small cocktail cabinet. Ace pulled off his topcoat and hat and threw himself thankfully into an armchair. He was in a soiled shirt and pants — no more. In the light of the reading lamp his square face was blue round the jaws for want of a shave and he needed a haircut.

Gloria brought him a drink over. He took it. Then caught her arm and dragged her down on to his lap. Being still only in her negligée and pyjamas, her soft flesh felt warm and comfortable against him.

'Tell me what's been happening to you, kid,' he murmured 'An' you don't hafta hide anything. You've got me with you now. I'll take care of you.'

Gloria wriggled a trifle but he did not let her go. His arm stole round her waist and held her firmly. By degrees, because there was nothing else she could do, she told him her story — as far as she wanted him to know it. He had finished his drink by the time it was over.

'So you took that skunk 'Fingers' for protection, did you?' he asked grimly. 'An' this is what you got?'

'This is what I got,' she agreed. 'I sort of had an idea you might see the

218

newspaper headlines and try and find me.'

'Your idea was right, kid. When I like a dame, I stick by her, see — unless she gives me the double-cross, then I sorta forget what I'm doing.'

'What about that fence in Harrisburg?' she asked. 'Did you get him?'

'Not yet. The heat's still on. Mebbe a couple of weeks before I can risk it.'

'Then where are those jewels you took? Sure they're safe?'

Ace grinned widely. 'Stitched into that overcoat, baby — all of 'em; or anyway, as many of 'em as survived that motor crack-up we had. I got friends who got me the coat; the rest I did myself. An' I've been thinking — '

Gloria waited while he mused. His free hand was stroking her knee absently.

'Suppose you an' me blew town together?' he murmured. He cuddled her up against him so she could hardly move. 'We could get across to California. I could fix it. I got friends, like I told you, an' once I've sold my rock-pile, you an' me can live like that guy Rockefeller.'

'Yes, but — what about 'Fingers'? I thought you were going to take care of him? You won't if we get out of town altogether, will you?'

'I'll fix him before we go. I've got it all doped out.'

Gloria said nothing. She was trying to imagine why Ace was here, with no police after him. She was also struggling to think of a way by which she might reach the phone and tip off headquarters that now was their chance.

'I — I'll get you another drink,' she said, and had fought her way from Ace's lap before he could offer any protest.

He looked after her sleepily as she went over to the cocktail cabinet.

'You haven't answered me, kid,' he reminded her. 'Are you willin' to take a gamble with me an get outa town?'

'Yes — of course I am. But we can't go right now. You need rest, one thing. You're all in. Take a sleep.'

She went back to him with the drink and dodged his arm as he tried to draw her down to him again. He took the glass and stared at her.

'What's the matter, kid? Don't you like the way I hold you? Haven't lost my touch, have I?'

'Of course not. Try and rest, Ace, then we'll figure things out. You know I'm with you, right to the end of the line.'

'Yeah — ' He reflected over this while Gloria's eyes strayed to the two automatics he had in his pants belt — one her own and the other his. 'Yeah, sure you are.'

Half stupefied by the drinks he'd had, which had come on top of an empty stomach, and worn out anyway from his exertions and nervous strain, his eyelids began to droop. Gloria gently took the glass from his fingers and stood looking at him. Then she went over to the armchair opposite and sat down, watching. At last Ace's head began to slump forward.

She got up and went silently towards him, reaching for the automatics. He stirred a little as she came near, and she promptly jumped back. Finally she decided that it was too long a risk to take to get the automatics so, instead, she went to the telephone, raised it gently, and dialed.

'Get me police headquarters,' she muttered into the transmitter. 'Sixth precinct — Captain McArdel, of the Homicide Division.'

There was a pause, then a voice answered. Gloria spoke again in a low tone. 'That Sixth precinct? This is — '

She stopped dead. Abruptly, Ace had jerked up his head and snatched out his own automatic. He leveled it at her steadily, then he motioned for her to put the phone down. Very slowly she did so, staring at him.

'Took me for a sucker, huh?' he asked deliberately.

'I — I thought I — '

'I know what you thought, kid — that I was asleep. I was fooling, see? That's me — always smart. Don't take risks before I'm sure. I figgered you were on the up-an'-up with me, but I took care to make sure. Good thing I did. Tried to sell me out to the cops, didn't you, Gloria?'

Gloria did not move. Ace got on his feet and came over to her, his face set and ugly. He stopped within a foot of her, the gun pointed.

'Remember me sayin' I kinda forget what I'm doin' when a dame double-crosses me?'

'Wait a minute. Ace. You've got this whole thing wrong — '

'No I ain't. You played me for a sucker — had me thinkin' you meant it. I've been through what I have to get to you, an' this is how you hand it back to me — by tryin' to get the police. They'll wonder why your call cut off like it did; they'll trace the number, an' then case the place, maybe. They won't find me; but I guess they'll find you. I'm goin' to let you have it, kid — '

He swung at that moment at a sound from the window. A figure leapt in and dived low as Ace fired. The girl jumped away quickly, her eyes wide at the sight of 'Fingers' hurtling suddenly across the room. Up came his fist, knocking Ace spinning before he could fire again.

As he crashed into the divan and then tumbled over the back of it, the automatic in Ace's belt dislodged, though he still kept his own in his hand, until 'Fingers' blasted it from his grip with livid fire from his own automatic.

Gloria hurtled forward to get her own gun from the divan, but 'Fingers' whirled out his arm and stopped her. Stumbling backwards she collided with the reading lamp and nearly knocked it over. Breathless, she stood up again and watched.

Ace, bereft of weapons, kept low down behind the, divan; then, when 'Fingers' made the mistake of leaning over it, he found himself seized round the back of the neck, dragged down, and pounded with a murderous; fist. He dropped his gun and it bounced well under the divan out of reach.

After that, it seemed to Gloria that a whirlwind had struck the place. Both men got on their feet and began slamming into each other with all the strength they possessed. They hit the walls, knocked the table over, smashed the glass front of the bookcase and finished up with the rug half wrapped around them. 'Fingers' was the first to get up dragging Ace with him.

'Now, start talking!' 'Fingers' panted, and brought his fist round into Ace's battered face with demoniacal force. 'Where's that rock pile? Come on, damn you! There's no time to waste!'

Ace shook his head dazedly, hardly aware of what he was doing. Blows rained again, spinning him backwards towards the open window. A final uppercut sent him hurtling out blindly on to the fire escape, where he lay, gasping for breath

'Fingers' hesitated, and then swung back on Gloria. Just in time, he grabbed her as she felt frenziedly under the divan for the automatic.

'No, you don't sweetheart. I've plenty to settle with you! Remember that I told you I'd take care of you one day? I aim to do that right now. Nothing fancy. Just straight through the heart. I can always get the slug out afterwards, so's nobody can trace it.'

Gloria backed away. 'Fingers' had his automatic firmly gripped. He followed Gloria up, keeping his eyes so fixed on her that he didn't look behind him; didn't see the bruised, blood-streaked Ace sidle over the window ledge and to the floor.

'Before I finish you.' 'Fingers' said, 'it's

just possible you might know where Ace put his stuff. How about it?'

'She can tell you, 'Fingers', but it won't do you any good!' Ace snapped.

'Fingers' wheeled round to see him looking over the top of the divan. He fired simultaneously with the automatic he had dug out from under the divan's springs. 'Fingers' lurched. Ace fired again — and that finished it. 'Fingers' dropped heavily, his gun tumbling from his hand.

'I guess that settles it,' Ace said bitterly, heaving on to his feet. 'I've been wanting to put a slug in that guy for years, an' now I've done it. An' I've that double-cross of yours to take care of, sweetheart, right now.'

'Not now, or any other time, Ace,' said a voice from the fire escape and, a second later, Captain McArdel stepped into the room with two officers, all of them with their guns ready.

'Thank heaven you got here, Captain!' Gloria said breathlessly. 'I'd begun to think the police were fast asleep.'

McArdel said nothing for a moment. He watched as Ace was disarmed, then he turned to the girl.

'Ace pulled a fast one, Miss Vane,' he explained. 'We thought he'd go to 'Fingers' place first, but he did some trickery with Toni, the head waiter. What got us moving was Toni's return to the 'Silver Slipper' — obviously to tell his boss some news — and then 'Fingers' hasty departure afterwards. We followed him, and there it is. Had we been a bit sooner, we could probably have stopped Ace committing yet another murder.'

'I ain't worryin',' Ace said sourly. 'It'll be a pleasure to fry for a skunk like 'Fingers' was — and the rest of them that I bumped off don't matter. Anyway, there ain't much fun left in livin'. Gloria's turned sour on me, an' you mugs have me pinned.'

'His jewelry and stuff are in his overcoat,' Gloria said quickly and the Captain nodded.

'Women!' Ace said with contempt. 'Cheat you to the last! Except for a little number I've been around with lately.'

'If you mean Anna Drew, fella, you can forget her,' McArdel said. 'Our boys saw her take Toni away in the car, and we're bringing her in for questioning. She seems a queer sort of a chauffeuse, to say the least.'

'She's a small-time thief!' Ace snapped venomously 'She'll talk if you make her; 'bout time somebody took a bastin', besides me!'

McArdel shrugged and turned aside to the overcoat patting it quickly. He nodded and put it over his arm.

As he turned to the door with Ace and the two officers in front of him, he looked back at Gloria.

'What I said, Miss Vane, still holds good,' he remarked. 'Get out of this city and out of this State; you will find it safer. Ace and 'Fingers' both have men loyal to them. They may make it tough for you. Get out, whilst you can.'

'First thing tomorrow,' Gloria promised. 'Teeth or no teeth!'

We do hope that you have enjoyed reading this large print book.

Did you know that all of our titles are available for purchase?

We publish a wide range of high quality large print books including:
Romances, Mysteries, Classics
General Fiction
Non Fiction and Westerns

Special interest titles available in large print are:
The Little Oxford Dictionary
Music Book, Song Book
Hymn Book, Service Book

Also available from us courtesy of Oxford University Press:
Young Readers' Dictionary
(large print edition)
Young Readers' Thesaurus
(large print edition)

For further information or a free brochure, please contact us at:
Ulverscroft Large Print Books Ltd.,
The Green, Bradgate Road, Anstey,
Leicester, LE7 7FU, England.
Tel: (00 44) **0116 236 4325**
Fax: (00 44) **0116 234 0205**

Other titles in the
Linford Mystery Library:

THE RESURRECTED MAN

E. C. Tubb

After abandoning his ship, space pilot Captain Baron dies in space, his body frozen and perfectly preserved. Five years later, doctors Le Maitre and Whitney, restore him to life using an experimental surgical technique. However, returning to Earth, Baron realises that now being legally dead, his only asset is the novelty of being a Resurrected Man. And, being ruthlessly exploited as such, he commits murder — but Inspector McMillan and his team discover that Baron is no longer quite human . . .

DEVIL'S PEAK

Brian Ball

Stranded in a High Peak transport café during a freak snowstorm, Jerry Howard finds himself in a vortex of Satanism. Brenda was a motorway girl with a strange scar on her back. The Mark of the Beast. She knew the history of the Brindley legend. And she alone knew the rites. She had been on Devil's Peak before. Now it was Walpurgisnacht and the horned goat was expected. Events moved to a horrendous climax . . .

DEATH ON DORADO

John Light

When wealthy businessman Edlin Borrowitch is murdered, Tec Sarn Denson is called in to defend the woman accused of the killing, Ros Kernwell. The case is a puzzling one and Denson finds her innocence difficult to prove. However, the one thing he doesn't lack is a list of suspects — but when everyone has a motive for murder, how can he choose? And how can he stay alive when the murderer is out to get him too?